In the SHADOWS of ROME

The
PHANTOM
of the
COLOSSEUM

To Thibault,
faithful proofreader,
principal advisor,
and wonderful husband.

Under the direction of Romain Lizé, CEO, MAGNIFICAT
Editor, MAGNIFICAT: Isabelle Galmiche
Editor, Ignatius: Vivian Dudro
Proofreader: Kathleen Hollenbeck, Samuel Wigutow
Layout Designers: Élisabeth Hebert, Magali Meunier
Layout: Text'Oh
Production: Thierry Dubus, Sabine Marioni

In the SHADOWS of ROME

The
PHAN**T**OM
of the
COLOSSEUM

Sophie de Mullenheim

Translated by
Janet Chevrier

M<small>AGNIFICAT</small> · Ignatius

CONTENTS

Martyr (from the Greek *martus*, "witness"). Literally a martyr is someone who testifies to his faith. However, the word is mostly used by the Church for those who died for their faith. More commonly, a martyr is someone who suffers persecution for his faith.

PROLOGUE

Thump! Thump! Thump! The banging on the door was enough to shake the walls of the whole villa.

"Open up!"

Blandula jumped and dropped her master's hand. She had been massaging his fingers with perfumed oils, for old Cornelius suffered from arthritis. His joints were swollen and gnarled with age.

"Open up!"

Blandula shot a worried look at her master. But he just smiled at her and said, "Go quickly, my child. It's me they are after."

But the girl didn't budge. In the rooms nearby, she could hear the other servants gathering up the last of their belongings, dropping things in their panic. She could hear stifled weeping.

"Go, Blandula!" Cornelius repeated. "You are free now."

Master Cornelius had granted freedom to Blandula and all the other slaves in the household just a few days before. He had offered them their liberty as though he knew that he would soon be deprived of his. Many of them had already left. The last ones were about to flee.

Master Cornelius got up slowly and went to the front door. He held himself completely upright, with dignity. He was not afraid. He had been expecting this day for a long time.

"Open up, or I'll—"

Before the soldier could finish his sentence, the master of the house opened the door. Calmly looking the soldier in the eye, he said, "What can I do for you?"

The soldier didn't bother to answer. He stepped forward, grabbed poor Cornelius by the shoulder, and, without ceremony, shoved him back into the room. Blandula, who had followed her master, choked back a cry.

"Filthy Christian!" said the soldier. "You know very well why I'm here!" He signaled for his men to enter and commanded, "Search everything!"

The men spread out into all the rooms, knocking everything over and turning everything upside down. Blandula trembled at each thud, wincing at the sound of every object that fell and shattered.

"There's no need to ransack everything," Cornelius said calmly after a few minutes. "It's me you want."

The captain of the guard stretched out his arm and slapped the old man, saying, "I didn't give you permission to speak!"

Cornelius staggered under the blow but kept standing. He raised his eyes and caught the look of terror on Blandula's face. He smiled at her. Then he closed his eyes, and the girl could see his lips silently moving. Her old master was praying. His house was being ransacked, his life was in danger, and he was praying!

"What are you doing?" thundered the officer.

Cornelius opened his eyes and stared at him in silence.

"What are you doing?"

Still no reply.

The soldier became wild with rage. He grabbed the old man and forced him to his knees before him. Cornelius tried to resist, but in vain.

"Renounce your faith!" the soldier shouted.

Blandula's master breathed not a word.

"Renounce it!"

He gave the old man a kick in the stomach. Cornelius collapsed to the ground but still clenched his jaw.

"If you obey, your life will be spared," the officer whispered in honeyed tones.

But his words met with silence. The man continued to strike Cornelius. Another soldier came in and started spitting at Cornelius and insulting him.

Cornelius struggled to raise his head. Blandula trembled, seeing blood flowing from his forehead. He looked from one soldier to the other. His jaw twitched, and he slowly said, "I believe…"

The two soldiers began to smile smugly, until he continued, "I believe in Jesus Christ, who rose from the dead!"

At this, they showered Cornelius with blows. Blandula shut her eyes tightly; this was more than she could bear. Suddenly there was silence. Blandula opened her eyes and gasped. The men were taking her master away!

"Master Cornelius!"

Despite everything, the old man turned and smiled at her.

"Do not be afraid, Blandula; nothing will happen to you. You are free now, my child. Flee!"

But the girl didn't move as the soldiers put her master in chains. After they set off with Cornelius, she went sadly to the doorstep and watched her master limp away. His white toga, spattered with blood, flapped pathetically around his thin legs. They hadn't allowed him to put on his sandals; he was barefoot. The emperor's men couldn't care less about his great age or honored position. The girl's heart broke as she watched them disappear around the street corner.

"Master Cornelius…" she murmured, with tears in her eyes.

In the neighboring wealthy villas, people kept out of sight. Blandula could just make out a few figures at the windows, hiding in the shadows.

Not one neighbor had dared to defend the old magistrate. And yet, he was one of their friends. Master Cornelius had always been kind and courteous to everyone, charitable to the poor, always ready to listen. But at the start of this year, A.D. 303, it wasn't wise to defend a Christian. A person might get away with knowing one, but to go to his aid—that was much too dangerous. Emperor Diocletian had confiscated all the churches and banned any books that referred to Jesus Christ. Anyone who refused to worship the Roman gods was arrested. Anyone who proclaimed faith in the risen Christ was removed from the army and the government.

At last, Blandula turned and went back inside. The girl wandered through the deserted villa. The silence that reigned throughout the vast dwelling was frightening. Blandula mechanically began gathering up the objects the guards had thrown to the floor—the smashed vases, the ripped-open cushions, the headless statuettes. She tidied up her master's bedroom, secretly hoping that it would somehow bring him back. At the foot of the bed, she noticed an object that was dearer to Cornelius than any other. It was a scroll of handwritten pages rolled around two wooden rods. It must have slipped to the floor without the soldiers seeing it. If they had, they would have destroyed it.

"Those are the Gospels, Blandula," he had told her one day. "That book saved me."

The young slave girl sighed. Her master had been mistaken, she thought. Surely that book had been his downfall.

I

EVIL OMENS

Titus joined his friends, looking gloomy.

"Is something wrong?" Maximus asked him.

"The omens aren't good!"

With a sneer, Maximus looked at the man his friend had just left. The man's toga was frayed, his sandals scuffed, his fingernails dirty, his beard scraggly, and his hair unkempt.

"Unbelievable," Maximus said to his friend. "You're intelligent; how can you let that fraud dupe you like that?"

Nearby, the man in question was counting his coins with a satisfied smile, before going off to lure another passerby.

"He's a charlatan!" Maximus continued. "He's no more a seer than I am!"

"Don't be so sure," Titus said defensively. "He interpreted my dream very well."

"And...?"

"I don't like what he said. He told me I would meet a phantom today."

"Hold on—a phantom? Last time it was the ghost of a pharaoh who was trying to contact you!"

Titus shrugged his shoulders and pensively stroked his little monkey, Dux, nestling on his neck. "You don't understand anything," he grumbled.

Like many Romans, Titus was superstitious. When he was born, his parents rattled little bells around him to ward off evil spirits. In the morning, he never stepped out of the house on his left foot. If anyone spoke the words of an evil omen in his presence, he would spit on the ground three times.

"Well," replied Maximus, "I hope it did not spoil your appetite. Because I'm neither a phantom nor a pure spirit, and I'm dying of hunger!"

By his side, his slave Aghiles agreed with a nod. He and Titus followed Maximus as he headed straight for a street vendor who was trying to protect his tiny stall from the crowd. If a careless passerby knocked over his big steaming stewpot balanced on a little wooden stand, his earnings for the day would be lost.

It was without doubt the busiest time of day. Anyone would think the whole city was there at the Roman Forum. It was noisy. It was terribly smelly. People jostled one another, pushing to get ahead and treading on toes. Street vendors were hawking their wares at the top of their lungs: dried fruits, small game fresh from the hunt, garlic bread, fish, sausages dripping with fat, and fresh produce, as well as household items like oil lamps and cheap pottery. You could find anything at the Forum, including the occasional acrobats, animal trainers, and phony seers who were ready to part people from their money.

"We'll take a few sausages and some of your stew, please," Maximus shouted to the man guarding his pot, whom he knew well.

The vendor opened his stewpot and dipped in a ladle. The strong aroma of chickpeas and meat rose from the cauldron.

"The finest cook in the Forum!" exclaimed Maximus as he grabbed hold of the steaming bowl. He also took some bread rubbed with garlic. After Titus and Aghiles placed their orders, Maximus settled the bill.

"Thank you, Maximus!" said the vendor with a bow. "May your family be blessed by Jupiter and all the gods!"

Maximus bowed in return. "I'll bring the bowls back," he shouted as he left the stall. "We'll move away from the crowd; it's stifling here!"

If it were anyone else, the stew vendor would have refused. So many of his customers took advantage of the hubbub to steal his bowls, chipped as they were. But he had known the son of Senator Julius Claudius for years—he was an honest kid. He could trust him. And even if Maximus forgot to return his property, he knew where to find his father to get his money back. Julius Claudius was a just man; he always paid what was owed without complaint. More than that, he was generous. The senator knew how difficult it was for the poor to make a living in Rome. He always aided those who came to him for help.

The three boys found a relatively calm spot in the shadow of an arcade of the Colosseum, the biggest and most beautiful amphitheater in Rome. They sat down with their backs leaning against the great portal. With that, Dux came scampering down from Titus' neck to steal a piece of his bread.

"Hey, Dux!" Titus shouted. "Give that back!"

But the little monkey just looked at his master with a glint in his eye. He climbed a few yards farther up to sit on top of the arcade to enjoy his plunder in peace.

"That monkey is such a scamp! And to think, I once believed I would be his master!"

Titus' father was a wild animal dealer renowned throughout the entire city. Last year, for Titus' thirteenth birthday, he gave him a little monkey. The boy immediately named him Dux, which means "general," because Titus was proud to be able to give orders to an army officer. But things didn't quite work out as expected: Dux lived up to his name—for it was he who gave the orders! He was disobedient, mischievous, thieving, and gluttonous, but Titus and he were inseparable. Wherever Titus went, his monkey went with him, perched on his shoulder.

Let's linger a moment with these three friends as they have lunch in the shadow of the Colosseum.

The biggest and strongest, almost a giant compared to the other two, was Aghiles. He was forced into slavery in Numidia, in North Africa. He had dark skin, tightly curled dark hair, and eyes of deepest ebony. Not knowing his exact age, he guessed that he was sixteen or seventeen. The only thing he knew about his birth is that it had occurred the day his father killed a lion. That's why he was named Aghiles, which in his native Berber language means "young lion."

Aghiles had entered Maximus' service just a few months before. He was a present for Maximus' fifteenth birthday—his first slave. Since then, he had also become his best friend. He was loyal, solid as a rock, unflappable, and incredibly strong.

Aghiles could not have been more dissimilar from Maximus, whose build was far from what his name might suggest. As a baby, Maximus had been very big, chubby, and full of energy. "A true force of nature!" exclaimed the women who assisted at his birth. So naturally, and with great pride, his father named him Maximus. His son promised to be remarkable! Yet Maximus quickly lost his baby fat and lagged in size. He was rather small for his age and skinny, with very light blue eyes, an ever-pale complexion, and hair so blond it was almost white. But appearances are sometimes deceiving. Maximus was hardly ever ill, was a fast runner, ate like there was no tomorrow, and was afraid of almost nothing. He made up for his *minimus* stature with his incredible energy, a rare intelligence that some-times made him seem a little uppity, and an enormous appetite for adventure.

Titus, for his part, was of an entirely average height and weight for fourteen. His round face, framed by curly chestnut hair, exuded a zest for life. Although he was superstitious and fainthearted, he displayed great poise, but he also had a short fuse. Of the three, he was the smooth talker, the one who would give his opinion and make suggestions but who feared carrying them out. Due to his father's fame, he knew many people in Rome. Between his connections and his own ingenuity, he could work out a solution to most any problem.

"What bugs me about these divinations is their lack of detail," said Titus, thinking out loud.

"Sorry?" said Maximus, who had been keenly watching an acrobat in white make-up balancing on a tightrope.

"I was saying that the divinations are always too vague."

"Seers are crooks, but they're not stupid."

"What do you mean?"

"If a seer foretells something too precise," explained Maximus, "he runs the risk that it will never happen. But if he remains vague, you can interpret it however you like."

Maximus pointed to the tightrope walker and said, "Take him, for example. Who's to say that he's not your phantom?"

Titus looked at the tightrope walker and sighed. "Why can you never take these predictions seriously?"

"Why should I?" asked Maximus.

Titus frowned and fingered the round amulet he always wore around his neck to ward off evil spirits. It was no use talking to his friend about this subject, he thought, they would never agree.

Titus worshiped all the Roman gods with devotion and consulted the oracles, while Maximus was happy just to make a few offerings to his family's household gods. He thought that was quite enough. As for the oracles, he didn't trust them. To his mind, they were worthless, or worse, dangerous. By trying to know too much about what the future held, people lost all judgment and all freedom to act as they saw fit, he noticed.

Maximus could see that his friend was worried, and he wondered if this phantom business was going to ruin their whole day.

II

STOP! THIEF!

Suddenly a little boy darted toward Titus, snatched the amulet from around his neck, and ran off at full speed.

"Come back here, you horrible brat!" shouted Titus, waving his fist in the air.

Aghiles and Maximus jumped to their feet, their lunches crashing to the ground, and ran after the boy.

"Stop him!" yelled Titus after his friends. "Thief! Stop!" he shouted to the people round about. But his cries were lost in the clamor of the crowd. At that time of day, the Forum was buzzing with noise. People were shouting, chatting, and arguing. The air was filled with people calling out to one another, singing, and reciting poetry, to say nothing of the clatter of pots and pans and the occasional crash of merchandise tumbling to the ground. Amid all this racket, it was impossible to distinguish one conversation from another or to hear anyone shouting.

As Maximus and Aghiles disappeared into the crowd, Titus ran after them, shouting, "Hey! Wait for me!" He felt something jump on his back and climb to his shoulder. Dux had scrambled down from the arcade to join the chase.

The little thief was zigzagging at full tilt through the crowd. Aghiles had more trouble making his way through the forest of people. He bumped into the men and the women in his path, knocked over a few stalls, sent baskets of fruit flying, and was yelled at from all sides. Right behind him, Maximus tried to calm down the people as best he could. He quickly picked up some of the toppled trestles, caught a tottering woman, and offered apologies left and right as he followed on the heels of his friend.

Titus caught up with him, still shouting at the thief even though he was now too far away to hear him. "Give me back my *bulla*, you viper! May Jupiter strike you with a lightning bolt! May you roast in hell!"

Titus was enormously attached to that *bulla*. It had been a gift on the day of his birth, and he hadn't gone a day without it. Of course, as a baby, the amulet had been too big for him to wear, but his parents pinned it to his swaddling clothes. Titus was convinced that, until now, it had protected him. Losing it would be like losing the protection of the gods. He had to get it back.

Aghiles suddenly stopped. He scanned the crowd, looking around in every direction. One street led off the Colosseum square. Had the little thief gone that way? Or had he doubled back to hide among the crowd?

Maximus and Titus caught up with their friend.

"Did you lose him?" Titus asked, out of breath.

Aghiles motioned for him to keep quiet and squinted. Taller than most Romans, he could see over the heads of many people in the crowd. He peered in every direction, hoping he would spot something.

"There he is," he said, pointing to where people seemed to be moving apart to let someone pass. "This way!" he shouted.

He sprinted off again, and Maximus and Titus blundered blindly behind him, trusting their friend and his instincts.

The three boys ran down a street and then into a less crowded one. The figure of the little thief was disappearing to the left at the next corner. Aghiles sped up. When he got to the street corner, he hesitated, looked behind him, and then scanned the street before him.

Titus and Maximus joined him. They, too, looked down the street, busy with a few pedestrians: men, women, an old man… but no little thief.

"That's not possible!" said Titus. "He went this way. I saw him. By all the gods, Aghiles, you almost had him! It's like he vanished into thin air."

"Perhaps he's a phantom?" Maximus mocked.

"You're not funny!" shouted Titus. "He's stolen my *bulla*!"

"Maybe he's hiding somewhere," suggested Maximus. "It's the only explanation."

A spark of hope lit up in Titus' eyes. "But of course! He's hiding!"

The street was lined with tall buildings, their doors set back from the street under porches supported by pillars that made great hiding places. Titus ran to the first entranceway and inspected it; then he turned to his friends, shaking his head. He went to the second. Maximus and Aghiles followed close behind him, keeping an eye on the street ahead of him while he searched. If the thief felt in danger, he would surely spring out of his hideout. The boys would have to react swiftly.

Aghiles noticed an iron gate that had failed to interest Titus. He walked over to it and gave it a shake. The lock held secure, but the gate seemed loose; so he called the other boys.

"What is it?" Titus asked, as he and Maximus ran to him.

When Titus got there, he wrinkled his nose in disappointment. "Oh, that's just the entrance to one of the tunnels to the

Colosseum," he said. "It's the passage my father uses to take his animals through on circus days."

Maximus looked toward the tunnel lost in the shadows and remarked, "It's the perfect hideout."

"As long as you have a key," Titus added.

Aghiles grabbed the gate and gave it another shake. This time it was clear that the bars were not securely attached at the bottom. By pushing on them, one could make a large enough space for someone to crawl through. Titus was amazed.

Maximus smiled, "I think a little visit is called for."

"No need," said Titus. "There's no one inside."

"And how do you explain the gate opening like that?"

"Maybe it just came loose over time."

Maximus frowned doubtfully.

"It's a real labyrinth in there," said Titus. "We won't find anything if we don't know what we're looking for."

"We're looking to catch your thief."

Titus unconsciously touched his tunic in the spot where his amulet would normally be. He felt practically naked without it. "But he could be anywhere in the hypogeum."

"The hypogeum?"

Titus smiled. Maximus was like all the other spectators at the Colosseum who never saw anything but the stone bleachers of the amphitheater. He, on the other hand, knew all its secrets. "It's the backstage of the Colosseum, its basements," he explained. "It's where they store the stage decor and the cages for the wild animals. It's also where the gladiators get ready and where the prisoners wait to learn their fate. It's a kind of miniature city beneath the theater."

"Just like I was saying," said Maximus.

"What?"

"It's the perfect place to hide."

22

Titus shrugged his shoulders. "If my thief is in there, I'm willing to bet we'll never find him."

"So what do we do now?" asked Aghiles impatiently.

"Let's get going!" shouted Maximus.

III

THE WELCOMING COMMITTEE

Maximus got down on all fours, squeezed through the opening, and slipped inside the tunnel. He shivered. The air was icy. The walls were damp.

Outside, Titus was still hesitating. "Are you sure…"

Aghiles put a hand on his shoulder and, without a word, pushed Titus downward. Dux jumped over the gate and leaped into the tunnel to Maximus.

"Well, if that's what the general orders…" muttered Titus. "I don't really have any choice." He squeezed through the gate and entered the tunnel.

Aghiles shot a last look behind him into the street to make sure no one had seen them. Then he too twisted himself into contortions to crawl through the gate and pulled the bars back into place behind him.

Maximus screwed up his eyes and looked to the end of the tunnel. He really couldn't see a thing. If only they had a light! He turned to Titus and asked, "Do you know where we should go?"

Titus smiled and threw his shoulders back. He liked it when his friends needed him. It made him feel important. "This is almost my second home," he said. "For now, we must just follow the tunnel. Dux!"

The little monkey let out a bit of a squeak and jumped on his master's shoulder. Titus patted his head, pleased as ever when he seemed to have a little authority over his pet.

The three friends slowly made their way through the tunnel, which became darker and darker until they could no longer see anything ahead of them. Maximus stretched out his hand to find his way along the wall, but he quickly withdrew it; the wall was cold and oozing slimy water. A chill ran up and down his spine. In front of him, Titus too was feeling his way along. He knew the place well, but that wasn't getting him very far. Tense and on the lookout, he was aware that danger could leap out at him at any moment. Luckily, the little monkey on his shoulder gave him some comfort. As for Aghiles, he was as undaunted as ever. Maximus sensed his silent presence behind him.

Suddenly, the ground changed beneath their feet. The dirt gave way to somewhat even stone paving.

"We're there!" Titus said with a sigh of relief.

"Where?" asked Maximus.

"In the hypogeum. Wait!"

A quick, sharp noise made Maximus jump. A spark burst into the darkness, then another, and another. It was Titus, who after the third spark brandished a lighted lamp with a smile of victory.

"My father always keeps an oil lamp and a firestarter here."

His voice echoed strangely in the empty space. He moved the lamp around, and its little flame sent shadows dancing across the walls. Disturbed by the light, bats came swooshing over the boys, who instinctively ducked.

"There's where the animals are held before entering the arena," Titus said in a lowered voice, shining the light on wooden animal cages lined up against the wall. They were open. And empty.

"This is spooky," whispered Maximus. "It's like being in a dungeon." He began to move forward when a disgusting smell rose to his nostrils, a mixture of rotten food and dried blood. "Yuck! Who could possibly live in here?"

Aghiles was getting impatient. "Which way do we go?" he asked.

Titus hesitated then said, "Let's start with the gladiators' quarters. It's the closest. If it were me, that's where I'd hi—"

Before he could finish his sentence, Dux let out an ear-piercing cry, leaped to the ground, and disappeared behind one of the doors. Then there was a stifled noise.

"It came from there!" shouted Aghiles. He started to run when the door slammed shut in his face, almost breaking his nose. That set his blood boiling. He struck out with his fist and banged on the wooden door, forcing it open. A boy hiding behind the door was startled. Before he could escape, he took one of Aghiles' punches right on the chin. He tottered and collapsed to the ground.

Titus rushed over. "Bravo, Aghiles!" he exclaimed. "You got him!" He leaned over the figure on the ground and raised his lamp to see the boy's face. His chin was already going black and blue. "But that's not him," he added with disappointment. "That's not my thief. This one's much older."

Just at that moment, an object flew within inches of his head and smashed against the wall, sending tiny shards of pottery in every direction. Aghiles immediately turned and rushed to the place the large jug had come from. At the same time, three boys surged out of the shadows and jumped at Maximus and Titus. Maximus was small and nimble. He dodged their fists and fought back, kicking the attackers in the shins. He was wearing strong hobnailed sandals, and each of his kicks drew cries of pain from his assailants. For his part, Titus defended himself by brandishing his lamp before him. He set the hair of one boy on fire and burned the hand of another. There was a smell like barbecued pork! All the while he shouted insults and threats to give himself courage: "You bunch of cowards! Were you hiding? Were you afraid? You like sneaky, underhand tactics? I'll introduce you to my father's crocodiles if you continue. Come on, come on! Who'd like to be the first to meet them?"

Tempers flared all around. Perched on his master's head, Dux joined in the taunting too. He rolled his big eyes and bared his razor-sharp fangs. Suddenly, one of the attackers sprang in front of Titus, looked him straight in the eye, and with a nasty smirk, puffed out his cheeks and blew out the lamp.

Titus gulped and cried, "Aghileeeesss!"

At the other end of the corridor, the Numidian had just pinned an attacker against the wall. He didn't know how many others there might be, but he could sense their presence. His hunter's instincts were heightened. He was aware of the slightest noise, the rapid breathing, the breath smelling of garlic, and the odor of sweat. Even without seeing, he was able to locate those around him, to shower them with punches while fending off theirs.

"Aghileeeesss!" Titus cried again.

The Numidian turned around and rushed toward the sound of his friend's voice.

"Titus! Maximus!" he called.

They both shouted to make their presence known in the dark and knelt down. They were used to that. It was usually the way their fights ended.

"Light!" Aghiles bellowed. He wasn't sure which way to go first.

Titus fumbled about and found the oil lamp that he had foolishly dropped when it went out. Just next to it, the ground was damp: some of the oil must have spilled out. Titus frowned, but he grabbed the lamp anyway. Fortunately, he had brought the firestarter with him.

Suddenly, a long whistle echoed through the galleries of the Colosseum, and the attackers ran away. By the time Titus relighted the lamp, the corridor was deserted. Even those who had been lying on the ground were gone. Their friends must have dragged them away.

Maximus was a little stunned. He sat on the floor and rubbed the back of his head, which had hit the stone wall and was throbbing with pain. Titus had gotten away with just a few bruises on his arms and legs.

Unsurprisingly, Aghiles showed no trace of having been in a brawl. "Let's go after them!" he said.

"No, let's get out of here!" said Maximus and Titus together.

IV

AN ULTIMATUM

"Idiot!" yelled the gang leader as he struck the little thief so hard that he tottered and fell flat on the floor. The man stood over the boy menacingly. He was a hulking figure, stocky and imposing. He had dark eyes, fleshy lips, and tiny ears. The boy pulled up his knees and shrank back in the dust.

"Why did you disobey orders, Victor?" demanded the man with his fist raised and ready to strike again.

"I, I…" Victor stammered.

"No snatch-and-grab! I made that very clear." The man gave Victor such a slap it made the young boy's head spin. Victor stifled a whimper and gritted his teeth. His eyes filled with tears, but he wouldn't cry. Not now.

The gang leader, known as Fulgur, pulled himself up to his full height and shot his steely gaze at each of the boys around him. They all held their breath and stared at their feet.

"No snatch-and-grab thefts! Got it?"

The boys nodded their heads in silence.

Fulgur turned and pointed his finger at Victor. "And you! You'll find them for me! I want to know where they are before they have time to start talking."

"Yes, Fulgur."

The boss did an about-face and went to the door. "By this evening!" he thundered over his shoulder.

Victor gulped. By this evening?! That only gave him a few hours or else…

Fulgur was violent. A bully. Someone with no scruples who ruled his gang of thieves through a reign of terror. He was feared. Hated. But worshiped too. Because without him, all these boys would have been long dead. Of hunger. Or in a fight. Or in prison. One by one, Fulgur had gathered them off the streets and trained them to work for him. Every day, they brought him back treasures. In exchange, they were fed and clothed, with a roof over their heads and a family of sorts.

Victor rose painfully to his feet. His cheek was throbbing. He gripped the *bulla* in his fist. He hadn't let it go since he had snatched it from that boy. That cursed *bulla*! If only it hadn't been so pretty. As soon as he saw it, he couldn't resist. He had only come across Fulgur in the road a short time ago. He didn't yet know all of his rules. Till then, he had managed to survive on little thefts like this. A bit of bread here, a bit of clothing there, or a coin if he was lucky.

He smoothed his tunic to restore a bit of composure in front of the other boys, who were all looking at him. He tied the *bulla* around his neck and left the room.

"Victor!"

He stopped and turned around.

"Don't go that way," a boy his own age warned him. "Never go out that way, in case there's a problem. We'll be seen, and Fulgur forbids it. You have to go out through the Ludus Magnus."

The boy felt through his tunic pockets and took out a coin. "Here, for the guard," he said. "Always have a few coins on you to pay him off." The boy smiled at Victor. "Don't worry; you'll learn."

V

DELIBERATIONS

"How many were there?" asked Maximus.

"At least six or seven," said Titus.

"More," said Aghiles. "And the one who whistled."

"Where did that come from?" Maximus asked Aghiles.

"Don't know. In any case, they were ready for us."

"It's no longer the case of just a stolen amulet now," said Maximus, still rubbing his head.

"And to think I thought the Colosseum was empty except during the games!" Titus said. "It's crazy! We may have fallen upon an underground organization."

"It's worth looking into," said Maximus.

Titus nodded his head. He was already picturing himself emerging triumphant from the Colosseum with a gang of small-time bandits in chains behind him. The emperor himself would be in admiration of his bravery.

"In any case, we won't get our hands on them sitting here," said Maximus.

The three boys had hung around the entrance to the tunnel for a long time. They had hoped to catch a glimpse of some bandits or to find out more about what was going on. True, several boys had walked by the iron gate, but no one had stopped. And no one had come out either.

"We won't see anything else today. They are suspicious," said Titus.

"We've got to take them by surprise," Aghiles added.

"How?" asked Titus.

"Are there any other passages into the Colosseum?" asked Maximus.

"Yes, the main entrance," said Titus with a bit of sarcasm. "But that's not exactly the most subtle…"

"Is there another tunnel, maybe?"

Titus shook his head. He explained that there was a passage between the Colosseum and the gladiators' barracks nearby: the Ludus Magnus. It allowed the men about to go into combat to enter the arena without being swarmed by the crowd. But to go that way, they would first need to enter the barracks, which was sheer madness. The barracks were home to the best fighters in the city, and gladiators were not known for their meekness. There was also the tunnel reserved for the emperor and the vestal virgins, the priestesses responsible for keeping vigil over the fire of the goddess Vesta. But that too was impossible to enter.

"No, there is no other way to get in," said Titus. "Unless…"

"Unless what?"

"No, it's too stupid."

"Tell us anyway," Maximus insisted.

"There are always the sewers."

Maximus smiled and said, "Now there's an idea!"

VI

A DUTY OF REMEMBRANCE

Blandula didn't know what she should do. She had been roaming up and down the streets of Rome all day with no luck. Everywhere she asked, she was either abruptly sent away or given contradictory replies. No one was interested in the fate of the Christians killed in the Colosseum a couple of days ago. Or rather, no one dared show any concern for those people. Fear had closed their mouths and their hearts. No one she came across was able to tell her where the martyrs' bodies had been taken.

There was only one place the girl hadn't dared go, where it was highly probable she would find the body of Master Cornelius. The catacombs: those cemeteries located outside the city of Rome. She had heard that Christians buried their dead there. Could Master Cornelius be buried in one of them?

Blandula was terrified at the idea of going there. In Rome, it wasn't wise to hang around the cemeteries. They were sinister places frequented by shady characters. Small-time bandits ruled there and shamelessly pillaged the tombs. Poor wretches would hurry there at night in the hope of finding a few leftovers from the funeral ceremonies. Some would even take the wilting flowers or chipped pots to resell the next day in the Forum. Blandula didn't feel brave enough to enter these places of horror and misery. And then, there were so many catacombs. Which one should she search?

Yet she was torn, for she owed it to her master to make sure he had received a decent burial. If he had not received the proper rites, she believed, the soul of Master Cornelius would never rest in peace.

VII

THE SEARCH

Victor groaned as he surveyed the huge Forum stretching before him. There were so many people! How could he possibly hope to track down the three boys here? It would be like looking for a needle in a haystack. Unless he got lucky. But Victor had never had much luck. He didn't know who his father was; he had been brought up by his mother, the slave of a rich but violent man who used and abused his staff. When his mother died from the man's ill-treatment, Victor fled before the master could either sell him or abuse him. He was ten years old. For months, he wandered the streets of Rome, stealing here and there to keep himself alive. Perhaps the day he met Fulgur was the only time the gods were with him: at last, he wasn't alone any more.

Victor recalled that the three boys had been eating lunch when he had snatched the *bulla* from them. They must surely have bought their lunch from one of the vendors here on the Forum. He went back to the place he had first seen them, under the Colosseum arcade. A dirty, flea-bitten dog had his nose stuck in a broken bowl, sniffing and greedily lapping up the remains. He must have found what was left of the boys' meal. Victor looked at all the stalls around him. There were at least a dozen selling soup, cold cuts, and all sorts of bread. It smelled so good, his stomach growled. Victor swallowed hard.

He approached the first street vendor and questioned him. "I'm looking for my friends," he said. "Have you perhaps seen them?"

The man looked at him with a glint in his eye. "Your friends?"

Victor nodded.

"They went that-a-way!" he replied mockingly.

Victor automatically looked in the direction he indicated and frowned. "There were three of them," he explained. "A big one and two smaller ones. With a monkey."

"A monkey?" The vendor shook his head. "No, sorry. Can't help you."

Victor thanked him and went on to the next stall, with no more success. Having asked all of the vendors closest to the Colosseum, he was ready to give up. He would never manage to find them.

He wandered among the crowd, asking people at random without much hope, when a man in a hurry jostled him. He was carrying an enormous stewpot piled up with dozens of dirty bowls.

"Hey, watch where you're going!" Victor said.

The man stopped a moment, mumbled his apologies, and went on his way. Victor watched him go and saw that he suddenly stopped right near the Colosseum. He put down his stewpot, gave a kick to a stray dog that ran off barking, and picked a bowl up from the ground. He went back to his stewpot, put the bowl in, and continued on his way. A brilliant idea suddenly struck Victor. He ran and with just a few strides caught up with the man and called to him: "Hey!"

But, with all the hubbub, the man couldn't hear him. He kept walking straight ahead.

"Hey, mister!"

The man jumped, looked at Victor, and wrinkled his brow, trying to remember where he had seen this boy before. Then he grumbled, "I've already said I'm sorry."

Victor walked along next to him. "It's not about that," he said. "I'm looking for my friends. We agreed to meet at the Forum, but I can't find them."

"So? That's none of my business."

Victor took a deep breath and began to bluff. "I know they always buy their lunch from you. There are three of them. A very big one and two smaller ones. With a monkey!"

A little light came on in the man's eyes but immediately gave way to a suspicious frown. As they walked, he took a good look at Victor from the corner of his eye. "Don't know them!" he said.

"Oh, come on," Victor insisted. "They're always telling me you make the best meals in the Forum."

Flattered, the man began to smile.

"And what's more," Victor added, "that your stew is always sold out when the others still have enough to last for hours."

"It's all a question of the seasoning," the man whispered.

"That's just what my friends told me."

"I'd been hoping they'd show me your stall, but now I can't find them. Did you see them today?"

The man nodded his head. He was no longer suspicious. "They came for lunch and took three of my bowls. But they never returned them."

Victor feigned astonishment. "That's odd. Have you any idea where they could have gone?"

The vendor shook his head. "No. But I'm off to see Senator Julius Claudius to get my money back for the bowls of his son and his friends."

Poker-faced, Victor took in this information.

"You can tell Maximus when you see him," the man added.

"Sure, sure, I'll do that."

The man mumbled something incomprehensible and went on his way.

Victor was jubilant. He let the man go but followed him at a distance. When he at last saw him stop before a sumptuous villa, it took just a matter of minutes to confirm what he suspected: this was the house of Senator Julius Claudius, the father of a certain Maximus.

Victor breathed a sigh of relief. Fulgur would have the information he was after. And by this evening, as demanded.

VIII

HALT!

Bent over, Titus was inspecting every little nook and cranny of the lane a few steps from the Colosseum. "I'm sure it's here somewhere," he said over his shoulder to his friends.

"Hurry up," Maximus urged him.

It was almost night. At the beginning of the year, the days were short and everyone hurried home early for the *cena*, the most important meal of the day. But Maximus, Aghiles, and Titus wouldn't be sitting down to supper anytime soon; they had more important things to do. They would make do with a few mouthfuls at home later. In any case, Maximus hated those endless meals. He liked to keep well away from the formal dinner parties that his father's position required. And if he was late coming home, he only had to say that he had been at Titus' house, while Titus would say he had been with Maximus. Their parents were so used to their being at each other's houses, they never even worried anymore about their absence. And the presence of Aghiles did a lot to reassure them. With the giant Numidian accompanying them everywhere, what could happen to them?

"There!" Titus exclaimed, pointing out a manhole cover barely visible by the light of the moon. It formed a narrow opening in the ground that linked a long rivulet to the city's network of sewers. It was where the rainwater drained off from the many floors of the great amphitheater. In the past, the network was also used to divert tons of water into the Colosseum itself to create a huge pool on which life-sized naval battles were staged. Both the emperor and the public adored them.

The passageway was narrow but large enough for the boys to squeeze through. But alas, there were two thick iron bars blocking the access.

"We'll have to pull them out," said Maximus. He shot a glance at Aghiles, who went to have a look. He positioned his hands on the two bars, dug his heels in against the wall, and pulled with all his might. Nothing budged.

Maximus studied the makeup of the wall more closely.

"We just need to scrape away the mortar to get the bar out. Do you have a knife?"

Titus and Aghiles both shook their heads.

"Maybe we could try with this?" suggested Titus.

He undid the large brooch holding his toga in place. It was a curved piece of metal set in scrollwork with a long, sturdy pin attached. Titus removed the pin and began scratching at the wall with it. The mortar crumbled and fell to the ground into a small pile of white powder.

"With a little patience and elbow grease…"

While Titus worked away at it, Maximus and Aghiles stood guard, each of them watching one end of the street.

"It's working!" yelled Titus as the first of the iron bars began to move.

Maximus rushed to him and clapped his hand over Titus' mouth.

"Shush! Are you mad? You'll get us found out!"

At the same moment, they spotted a bright glimmer of light at the end of the lane.

"A patrol!" whispered Maximus.

42

A group of armed soldiers had just come around the street corner. Several of them carried torches, sweeping the area around them with light.

Maximus cast his eye behind him, toward the other end of the street. Then he looked at Titus.

"How much more time do you need?"

"I won't get it done before they get here."

Maximus summed up the situation as quickly as he could. Their position was too visible. For now, they were in the shadows, but as soon as the guards approached with their torches, they would be discovered.

"We have no choice," he whispered, "we have to get out of here."

"And give up now?" asked Aghiles.

Maximus nodded. "For the moment, yes. This is no time to get caught. We'll come back later."

At that time, the soldiers were more on the lookout than ever. They had received orders to arrest all Christians, who often gathered at night to pray. In their eyes, anyone out late in the streets was suspect. Even Maximus' senator father wouldn't be able to stop his arrest if that was what the soldiers decided. For some time now, no one was too highly placed to escape the law. No one was above suspicion. What's more, many of the Christians arrested were themselves magistrates and patricians.

"But later might be too late," said Aghiles. "They'll get away. They'll sell the *bulla*. Keep going! I'll take out the guards."

Without waiting for his master's reply, he was off in the night in the direction of the patrol. Maximus tried to grab hold of his tunic, but Aghiles shook him off. Within seconds, he was within the soldiers' torchlight. He flexed his muscles and ran.

"Hey, you!" shouted the first soldier to spot him.

Crouching in the shadows, Titus and Maximus didn't know what to think. Their friend had run straight into the patrol. When he reached the first soldiers, he took advantage of their surprise, dodging one of them who was raising his sword, elbowing another, and pushing the last one out of the way with his arm. Aghiles was fast on his feet, and strong. In just a few strides, had had outmaneuvered the whole troop.

"Halt! Halt!" one of them shouted as he brandished his torch. "After him!"

The patrol turned around. Their weapons clanked as they rushed in pursuit of the culprit.

"Unbelievable!" whispered Titus in admiration.

Maximus was the first to get back to business.

"They could be back any moment. We've got to hurry!"

IX

THE MANHUNT

Aghiles ran with amazing ease. He came from a country where long-distance running was second nature. He would often run for miles before he and his whole family were captured and sold into slavery. Tonight, the Numidian far outdistanced his pursuers. His stride was easy, his breathing regular, his footing sure. They would never catch up with him. Once he was sure he had lost the patrol, he would go back to Maximus and Titus by another route, in the hope there would be no more surprises.

Aghiles hesitated at a crossroads. At night, all the streets looked the same, all the houses identical. But he mustn't make a mistake. He thought for a second before heading off to the left. If he turned right, he risked coming out into the Forum, where he would be exposed. What better than narrow little lanes to hide and protect him?

The noise of the patrol on his tail gradually faded, but Aghiles kept running. When at last he thought he had lost them, he began to slow down. He looked behind him, trying to see if they were still in pursuit. At that exact moment, a horse-drawn carriage turned into the street at a furious pace. In Rome, carriages had the right of passage at night, leaving the city to the pedestrians during the day. The driver saw the slave at the last minute. He pulled up on the reins. His horses jumped to the side just in time to avoid him. But the carriage swerved to the right and sideswiped Aghiles before continuing on its way without even stopping.

The shock sent Aghiles sprawling. When his head stopped spinning, he felt excruciating pain. He could tell his shoulder had been dislocated and his whole right side thoroughly skinned. He could feel his blood pulsing in his side. Aghiles painfully rose as best as he could, propping himself against a wall to avoid falling down again. Then he slowly stood up.

"There he is!" shouted a guard. The patrol was back on his track. They had just arrived at the end of the street and set off after him with renewed fury. This time, he wouldn't get away.

Aghiles cradled his shoulder in pain, gritted his teeth, and began running again. But his wounded side kept him from putting weight on his right leg. He was limping, and the stabbing pain was getting worse. Down a side street, he spotted a porch and ran to it. He plastered himself against the wall to disappear into the shadows and tried to catch his breath.

But the patrol, too, turned into the street. The soldiers kept running for a few yards and then stopped.

"I can't see him anymore," one of them yelled.

The clatter of weapons gave Aghiles a shiver. If the soldiers found him now, he was done for.

"That's impossible! He was limping!"

Silence fell. Aghiles closed his eyes. He held his breath. His heart was pounding so hard, he was afraid they could hear it.

"He's here; I can feel it. Search the street!" ordered the captain of the guard.

The Numidian readied himself. They would find him. It was only a matter of seconds. He was going to have to fight for it.

Suddenly, a hand grabbed Aghiles from behind and pulled him backwards.

X

THE SEWERS

After what seemed an eternity, Titus finally managed to undo the two bars blocking the entry to the underground passage. He turned around with a huge smile.

"There! That's it!"

He slipped his head into the opening but looked straight back up again.

"I can't see anything down there."

"We just need to follow the passageway. It can't be that complicated!"

Maximus glanced back at the street in the hope of seeing Aghiles returning. But the road was completely empty.

"Maybe we should wait for him a little longer," Titus suggested timidly.

The thought of continuing this adventure without his trusted friend by his side didn't fill Maximus with confidence. But he shook his head. "No, let's at least start to check out the layout. That'll give us a head start."

While Titus hesitated, Maximus forged ahead. Crouching down, bent in two, he managed to slip through the opening. He had to keep his head down, but it wasn't too difficult. He stepped forward a little to give Titus room to enter too.

Titus shivered and said, "We should have thought to bring torches with us."

"And risk being found out right away? No. We'll have to manage without light for now. Once we get into the Colosseum, there'll surely be some."

Titus raised his hand to his throat to grab his *bulla* and ask for the protection of the gods. But his lucky charm was long gone. That was enough to restore his determination. That cursed thief deserved to be caught and to pay for his crime!

"Let's go," he grumbled. "That thief will make a fine dinner for the lions!"

Just as they were about to climb into the darkness, a whimper stopped them.

"Dux?" Titus called.

A little cry answered from the opening above them.

"Come on, Dux, come!"

A few moments went by, but still no Dux. Titus went back to the end of the tunnel.

"Here Dux!"

It was no use. The monkey refused to obey.

"He's afraid of the dark."

Maximus sighed. That animal was really the limit. "Leave him outside," he suggested. "He'll wait for us."

Titus' eyes almost popped out at the very thought. "How can you even suggest such a thing!"

"General or not, I'm not letting a monkey order me about," said Maximus with exasperation. "May I remind you that it's your *bulla* we're looking for?"

Titus bowed his head, secretly cursing his monkey, and then slipped his hand inside his tunic. He took out a handful of seeds. He always had some with him to reward his pet when he was obedient. To be perfectly honest, he mainly used them to bribe him, but Titus would never admit that.

The monkey's reaction was immediate: the familiar sound of a handful of seeds drew him like a magnet. In a few leaps, he was by his master's side in the underground passage, eating greedily.

Since Titus was bent over, he couldn't jump onto his shoulder. So he slipped into the boy's tunic. Nice and warm. And also close to his stash of seeds.

"Okay, we're good to go," Titus shouted at last.

The two friends advanced carefully through the tunnel, treading in a little trickle of water. Their wet sandals squished like sponges, the sound echoing strangely in the confined space.

"We're lucky it hasn't rained lately," said Maximus. "This place must be like a mountain stream when it does."

He moved forward with outstretched arms, trying to make out the space before him. With each step, he checked the ground with his foot. They mustn't risk going too fast and falling into a well. Surely there would be several wells along the path of the sewers, to prevent floods of rainwater from suddenly inundating the streets.

The passage abruptly divided in two.

Maximus stopped and asked his friend, "Which way do you think we should go?"

"I don't know. To the right, I think…unless it's to the left…"

Maximus thought for several moments before saying, "Let's try to the right and see."

He advanced even more slowly, cursing the darkness as he went. The ground seemed slightly on an incline and a bit drier. Maximus bent down and picked up a few pebbles that he threw in front of him as he walked. With each, he strained his ear to hear its path. Suddenly he stopped.

"The ground goes down here and there's no more water. There must be a well nearby."

As he was speaking, Maximus threw another pebble and listened. The stone ricocheted off the wall and rolled on the ground. The path ahead of them seemed clear.

"It's a real labyrinth. I never realized. We must absolutely remember the way out. We took the first right turn. Don't forget!"

Titus nodded and knotted the right fold of his tunic to remember the right direction. But then…

XI

BLANDULA

Outside, the footsteps of the soldiers could be heard approaching. Aghiles stared at the girl before him. She put a finger to her lips and opened her eyes wide to tell him to keep silent.

"He can't just have disappeared!" growled one guard outside.

"It's as though he vanished into thin air," said a second.

"It's surely one of those cursed Christians," thundered a third. "They're capable of sorcery; I'm sure of it."

Aghiles listened to the men gathered just outside the door. He held his breath.

"We're wasting our time here!" exclaimed the captain of the guard.

The small group of soldiers grumbled in frustration.

Aghiles could see the glimmer of their torchlight through the crack under the door.

"Let's go!" shouted the captain.

The clatter of weapons signaled the departure of the troop. Aghiles leaned his head against the wall and closed his eyes with a sigh of relief. When he opened his eyes again, he smiled at the girl, who hadn't left his side.

"Thank you," he said simply in a lowered voice.

She put a finger to her lips again and signaled to him to follow her. Once they had moved away from the door, she at last relaxed a little.

"Thank you," Aghiles repeated, without taking his eyes off her.

She looked to be about his age, petite, and pretty. Her long brown hair was gathered in a bun at her neck, revealing a face with fine features and an olive complexion. Her green eyes glinted with a worried look. She stared at him for a long moment in silence before looking at his side.

"You're hurt?" she asked in a gentle voice. "Was it the soldiers?"

Aghiles shook his head. "I got run over by a carriage."

"I'll take care of it," she said simply.

She left him there while she went into another room. Aghiles looked around him. It was a big, richly decorated place. It looked a little like the home of his master, Senator Julius Claudius, Maximus' father. Aghiles hoped that everything had gone all right for his friends. If Maximus and Titus had gotten hurt, he would never forgive himself—and neither would the senator. He trusted him with his son's safety.

Aghiles gently felt his shoulder and tried to move his arm. It was painful, but nothing seemed to be broken. He closed his eyes, gritted his teeth, and rammed his shoulder against the wall.

Aghiles choked back a cry of pain, shook his head, and moved his arm around. There, that did it: his dislocated shoulder was back in place. Then he had a good look at his side. It wasn't a pretty sight. The wound was wide, and the top layer of his skin completely rubbed off. Aghiles cleaned it with a fold of his tunic, and then readjusted the cloth back over his side with a grimace of pain. As he did so, the girl reappeared.

"What are you doing?" she asked him.

"I have to go. My master may be in danger."

"Let me at least dress your wound."

Aghiles wrinkled his nose; he didn't have time. The girl smiled at him.

"You won't go as fast if your wound is hurting," she said. "Trust me. I'll be quick."

She pointed him to a sort of long bench pushed against the wall. Aghiles sighed and lay down on it. Now that he had stopped running and wasn't being chased any more, the pain came back, even worse.

The girl was as good as her word: she worked quickly. With expert hands, she applied boiled cabbage leaves to his wound and wrapped it with clean linen. Then she held the poultice firmly in place as she wrapped a wide band of cloth around Aghiles' waist. A gentle warmth immediately spread through the dressing. He sat up. In a few minutes, he wouldn't even feel it any more. He had always been tough.

"You're really badly banged up. If the soldiers find you…" Just the thought of it gave her the shivers. As Aghiles kept silent, she went on, "What's your name?"

"Aghiles."

"Aghiles… Why were they chasing you?"

He didn't reply.

"Are you one of them too?"

He wrinkled his brow and looked at her, wondering what she meant. Blandula hesitated. Her question was a little risky but she had, after all, already taken an enormous risk by helping him.

"Are you a Christian?" she asked, instinctively lowering her voice to a whisper.

"No."

"I just thought…the soldiers…" The girl needed to talk. She had felt so alone over the last several days. "They took away my master, Cornelius. He was a Christian."

53

"*Was?*"

Blandula lowered her head, and tears welled up in her eyes. "He was killed in the last games at the Colosseum. I wasn't there. They told me about it. And I don't know where they've taken him." Her voice broke.

Aghiles felt sheepish. He cleared his throat; he didn't know what to say. "Thank you..." he began.

"Blandula."

He looked at her, not understanding.

"My name is Blandula," she said.

Aghiles' eyes lit up with a smile. "Thank you... Blandula."

And she too smiled. But she could see Aghiles was in a hurry to go. She led him in silence through a maze of hallways. When they arrived before a small door, not the one he had entered, she explained, "This leads to the back of the villa. If the soldiers are waiting for you at the top of the street, they won't see you."

She opened the door slowly, took a quick look outside, and stepped back in. "It's okay, you can go. The street is empty."

He stepped past her in silence. He gave her a last nod of the head to thank her and went out. She was right: the coast was clear. He turned to smile at his pretty savior, but she had already quietly closed the door behind him.

Aghiles hesitated a moment, trying to get his bearings, before stepping back into the street. When he arrived at the corner of a larger road, he jumped back against the wall. Blandula was right again: a small group of soldiers was still lying in wait at the top of the street. Aghiles quickly checked out the surroundings, spotted a porch set back from the road, and ran for it. The guards didn't see him. From where they were, they wouldn't be able to spot him now. So Aghiles left his hiding place and rushed toward the Colosseum. He turned a corner and ran smack into a soldier who had stayed behind, probably to keep

54

watch. The Roman's eyes opened wide in astonishment. He recognized Aghiles and was about to cry out when Aghiles hit him hard on top of his head. The soldier tottered and fell. Aghiles tapped his shoulder with a smile: it was back in perfect working order!

There was no time to hang around. He hurried on his way, hoping to avoid any further encounters and get back to his friends as quickly as possible.

When he got back to the underground passage where he had left them, Aghiles was relieved to see the iron bars lying on the ground. He took a quick look around him before slipping down into the opening. He crawled forward on all fours, just as when he used to hunt game in the bush. The wound in his side was throbbing, but he kept going.

XII

A PASSAGEWAY

Maximus looked at Titus. It wasn't so dark here. He could see his friend's eyes sparkling with excitement. They had done it! In front of them, they could make out the long corridor of the hypogeum. They could take their enemies by surprise. Titus smiled at the thought of the fear they would strike in them. In his mind, there was no doubt that they would nab the thief and crush their assailants. Then they would only have to find Aghiles and things would all be wrapped up.

"Let's go back outside," whispered Maximus. "Aghiles will be looking for us; then we'll work out the best thing to do."

"It's not complicated. We've got to get going," said Titus, all excited. "We'll pull out their eyes, the hair on their legs, and the nails on their toes. And then throw them to the lions! No mercy!"

Maximus forced back a smile. Ever since he was a little kid, Titus had been immersed in the world of the circus games, a world of spectacle, of course, but cruel and merciless as well. His father was known for the ferocity of the wild animals he purchased, tended, and resold to those in search of a few thrills. His rhinoceroses would charge at the drop of a hat; his crocodiles had terrifying jaws; his tigers were strong and aggressive, and his buffalos, muscular. The only animals Titus' father didn't deal in were lions and elephants; trade in them was reserved for the emperor. Brought up in a world that thrived on a thirst for blood and violence, Titus' creativity had no limit when it came to torture. At every street fight, he would promise his enemies the worst kind of suffering and imagine the most terrible punishments. He would promise and imagine…but as soon as it came to actually doing anything, Titus immediately lost all his nerve and bravado.

"Let's go back," was all Maximus said.

The two boys slowly struggled back through the bowels of the sewers, and then retraced their steps. When they came to an intersection, Titus bent down to examine the base of the wall. Then he turned into a tunnel where he found the little heap of pebbles they had left there. It was an idea they had thought up to find their way back.

Suddenly, as they passed a corridor, he stopped.

"What is it?" asked Maximus.

"I hear a funny kind of noise," whispered Titus. "Could we have taken a wrong turn?"

Maximus too listened carefully. The noise suddenly seemed to be coming from all sides. It sounded like a million fingernails scratching on the stone.

"Aaaah!" screamed Titus. Something had just run between his feet. It was warm and furry. "Rats!"

Maximus could now clearly hear claws scraping the ground along with squeaking. He felt the fur and the whiskers of the vermin tickling his ankles. "Ugh. Dirty little animals! How disgusting!"

With a sharp kick, he sent one of them flying against the wall. The animal screeched in pain. Overcoming his disgust, Maximus struck out at anything that moved. Next to him, Titus was struggling to stay calm. Big animals were fine. But little ones like this, never! He clapped his hands and stamped his feet to chase the vermin away.

In panic, Dux, tucked nice and warm inside his master's tunic, lost his balance. He dropped the handful of seeds he had been nibbling on since the start of this expedition. With that, a swarm of rats rushed around Titus' feet to grab the precious bounty. "Help! They're attacking me!" he shouted.

The rats were climbing all over his feet looking for the seeds that had fallen on his sandals. Titus could feel their little claws on his skin, their whiskers, and even their teeth. He started hopping up and down and screaming. "Maximuuuus!"

His friend was still kicking with his sandals every which way. Sometimes he would stamp on the end of a tail, sometimes, something bigger. It cracked and it slithered under his feet! It was soft and slimy! Maximus felt like he was going to be sick. "Quick! I need air!" he yelled.

XIII

THE STAKEOUT

Fulgur's henchman carefully studied the surroundings. The villa of Senator Julius Claudius was located on a dead-end street. It was an ideal spot to lie in wait and take someone by surprise. But this man had a suspicious nature. He knew from experience that things were never as simple as they might seem. He needed to work out an escape strategy in case things got complicated—for instance, in case the boy who lived here was like that giant who had knocked out several of his gang! Fulgur had warned him: he wanted this job carried out without a hitch.

It was a dark night, but there was enough moonlight to make out the house fronts. A few were decorated with colonnades or statues that would be perfect to climb up and down from the terraced roofs. If he had to make his escape, that's what he would do. Since he had been living in hiding, Fulgur's henchman had developed good survival instincts. An extremely fast runner, he climbed like a monkey, and he had mastered all the martial arts, as well as ducking and diving. He was sharp, heartless, violent, unbending. A brute. If Fulgur had singled him out from all the others, it was for good reason.

Suddenly, there were hurried footsteps. The man shrank back into the shadows and readied his fists. He had to be quick. He would jump his victim, neutralize him, and threaten him.

Fulgur had forbidden him from killing the senator's son. That would risk setting the police on their tail, just what they didn't need. He must simply rough him up and frighten him enough to keep him quiet about what he saw in the Colosseum. And if he had already talked, to make him withdraw his witness statement.

The footsteps came closer. The bandit bent slightly forward. But just as he was about to leap out, he jumped back again. It was a woman who had just turned into the street. A slave, no doubt. With her head covered with a veil and her hand clutched to her chest, she was walking very quickly. She glanced behind her before knocking at the little door to the side of the senator's villa. It was immediately opened.

"Quick, come in, Flavia," whispered someone from behind the door, someone the man couldn't see from where he was. "Were you followed?"

The slave girl shook her head and disappeared inside.

XIV

REUNITED

The collision was violent and unexpected.

"Oof!" spluttered Aghiles.

Titus had just run into him at full speed. It was so dark, he hadn't seen him.

"Aghiles?!"

"Titus? Maximus?"

"I'm over here," answered Maximus. "And am I happy to see you again! I see they didn't catch you then."

"And you? Did you find anything?"

"Rats!" exclaimed Titus. "It's infested with rats!"

"Rats?" Aghiles' voice didn't betray any emotion, no disgust, no fear. He just took in the information, nothing more.

"They must have been attracted by the seeds Dux spilled as we went in," Maximus said.

"You think so?" Titus asked, suddenly very embarrassed.

"We need to get going," Aghiles said.

He hadn't dealt with a whole troop of soldiers just to stand around chatting about a few rodents.

"No, I think we should go home now," suggested Titus. "It's late."

"This is no time to give up," Aghiles said.

"I'm not giving up! I'm just saying we could wait until daylight."

"Oh, that's a great idea!" said Maximus sarcastically. "And then we can wave to all the passersby as we break into the sewers."

"We can be discreet," Titus said. "And besides, there won't be as many rats."

"I doubt that! At least at night you can't see them," said Maximus.

Titus shivered. Just the thought of them made him want to throw up.

Aghiles had had enough. "I'm going back to the manhole," he said and set off without waiting for an answer. He didn't leave Titus and Maximus much choice, and they followed after him.

Several long minutes later, when Aghiles could finally stand up again, he sighed with relief. The tall slave stretched his legs and flexed his shoulders to get rid of the crick in his neck.

"We're not far from the gladiators' quarters and the prisoners' cells," Titus pointed out. He too was relieved because they had not come across a single rat. "The place where my father keeps his animals is almost at the opposite end. The end where we came in before. Between here and there, they could be hiding anywhere."

The hypogeum was a sort of giant labyrinth. Of course, Titus knew it like the back of his hand, but he was clearly not the only one. The ones who had attacked them must know the place well. Maybe even better than he did.

"Steady does it," whispered Maximus. "We have to go carefully and quietly if we want to find out where they're hiding and how many there are."

"That's the problem," Aghiles agreed, "how many of them…"

"It's pointless to attack if we're clearly outnumbered," continued Maximus. "If we are, we'll just have to be cleverer than they are."

It was very dark in the hypogeum, but there were openings here and there that let in a little outside light. The bright light from an almost-full moon reached down into the bowels of the Colosseum through hatches and passageways leading to the center of the amphitheater. There were several lifts of various kinds to take the scenery and the animals up to the stage.

Titus stepped forward, his senses on the alert. Each time he came to an intersection or the doorway to a room, he stopped, took a deep breath, closed his eyes, and stuck his head around the wall. Sometimes he moved too quickly to see anything, and he would have to start his game of peek-a-boo all over again. But at this rate, it would take hours before they ever got to the other end of the Colosseum.

"Let's split up," Maximus suddenly suggested in a muffled voice. "It will be quicker that way. Aghiles, you take the corridor on the right. Titus, the one to the left, and I'll keep going straight ahead."

Titus looked down his assigned corridor and trembled.

"Not that one," he whimpered.

"Why not?"

"That's where the cells are, where they keep the prisoners who are about to die."

"So?"

"It's spooky, and it's surely haunted by the ghosts of those who were held there. You'd have to be crazy to hide out in there. That's the last place I would go."

"Well then," snapped Maximus, "you'll be sure not to run into anyone!"

His sharp tone didn't allow for any argument.

Titus sighed and started down the narrow corridor. There were three doorways, one after another. The first door was open; the other two stood ajar. The boy cautiously peeked his head around the first door. Nothing. The room was empty. Titus sighed with relief. He hated this! Outside the second one, he put his hand to the door and pulled it toward him with gritted teeth, hoping it wouldn't squeak. It scraped a little against the ground but opened easily and noiselessly. Immediately, an awful smell rose to his nostrils. It made him feel sick. It was a mixture of blood, sweat, filth, and urine. Titus took a step back, steadied himself against the cold wall of the corridor, and, with his eyes closed, took a gulp of air. When he had calmed down again, he grabbed a fold of his tunic and held it over his nose and mouth. Then, cautiously, he poked his head through the doorway.

A scream stuck in his throat. He wanted to step back, but he couldn't: he was frozen to the spot. When at last his body obeyed him, he jumped backward, banged his head on the doorpost, and ran back to the end of the corridor. He came face to face with Aghiles.

"I didn't find anything," said Aghiles. "What about you?"

But Titus had lost his tongue. He was trembling from head to foot.

Maximus joined them and stared at his friend in astonishment. Titus was as white as a sheet.

"Are you all right, Titus?"

Titus didn't reply. His eyes were wide with terror.

At last, he opened his mouth; he tried to speak. Finally, he gulped and stammered, "A...a...phantom!"

XV

NIGHTMARES

Blandula woke with a start. She was drenched in sweat. Her hair was pasted to her forehead, her hands were damp, and her heart was racing. For several nights now, she had been terrified by the same nightmare. It had been useless to try to shake it off; the same horrifying dream came back each night with a vengeance.

In her dream, she could see herself standing at a doorway as her master, Cornelius, turned to her for the last time, smiling, and saying to her, "Don't be afraid. Nothing will happen to you. It's me they're angry with."

Then the soldiers hustled him off without ceremony, pushing him before them, prodding him with their lances. They made him walk ahead in full daylight into the center of the arena where the hungry lions awaited him.

The crowd in the amphitheater was transfixed. Blandula was horrified. Among the spectators, she could recognize Master Cornelius' neighbors, his former slaves, and a few of his servants. They all had the same look full of hate and fear.

"Kill him! Kill him!" they shouted with raised fists.

The old man stepped forward, standing tall despite the wounds that covered his back, with an air of serenity, clear-eyed. He advanced without fear as he murmured a prayer.

At the moment they unleashed the wild beasts, Blandula turned her head away. She couldn't watch. She covered her ears. She couldn't listen to the excited cries of the crowd or the sound of her master's bones being crushed. She fell to her knees, broken with grief.

Suddenly, another wave of cries rose from the crowd.

"She's praying!" shouted a man. "She's a Christian too!"

"Put her to death! Kill her!"

With that, Blandula raised her eyes and, horrified, realized they were now after her. The soldiers menacingly advanced toward her. Behind them, the lions awaited, their jaws frothing.

"Noooo!" the girl screamed.

Then she woke up…

Blandula got up slowly, rubbing her eyes in an effort to rid them of the terrifying images of her nightmare. A neighbor had once told her about the martyrdom of his master. He had been among the very first Christians to die. After that, the executions continued for several days. These stories haunted Blandula. She would imagine a scene and then couldn't forget it. She went to bed later and later, and got up earlier and earlier, and in between she barely slept.

She wandered the deserted villa endlessly, jumping at the slightest suspicious noise. A shout, a knock on a door, a patrol passing by. A few hours earlier, when soldiers had come into the street, she had put her ear to the wooden door to hear if they had come for her. That was how she had heard the breathing of the young man hiding on the porch. She understood right away that he was in danger. She didn't stop to think, but opened the door to him—and saved his life. Master Cornelius would have done the same.

Blandula left her bedroom and went to the patio at the center of the house. Her master had had a fountain put in there. It's where he liked to sit and think. For some time too, it was where he went to pray.

Blandula sat on the edge of the fountain. She raised her eyes to the heavens and looked at the stars playing hide-and-seek in the clouds. Against the dark veil of the night, the stars seemed to shine more brightly. How could she be sure that her master really was up there, as he had hoped to be? How could she be sure he wasn't instead wandering aimlessly somewhere, along with other restless spirits?

XVI

A PHANTOM

In any other circumstances, Maximus would have been amused by his friend's terrified look. But not this time. As soon as Titus pronounced the word "phantom," Maximus remembered the prediction that had so worried his friend that afternoon. The crooked fortune-teller had told him he would meet a phantom that day, and now he was imagining one. "By Jupiter, Titus!" he said. "The man is a liar! Snap out of it and help us!"

Titus' face clouded over. He became even more pale. He had forgotten all about the seer's predictions that afternoon. He stammered, "I…I…there's a…I swear."

"If you don't stop this, I'll predict something else in your future: my fist in your face! No need to be a fortune-teller to tell you that!"

"But…"

"May I remind you that we're here because of *you*, because of YOUR *bulla*. So, either calm down or we forget the whole thing."

Titus shook his head without a word.

"Okay, let's go! If not, we'll be here all night."

Maximus took a few steps into the corridor. Looking back, he said, "It's lighter this way. I checked. There's no one here."

Aghiles followed his footsteps, and the two advanced together with determination. After a few yards, they turned around.

Titus wasn't following them. He was still standing there. He hadn't budged an inch. They could hardly see him anymore in the half-light.

"Titus!" Maximus called to him. That's strange, he thought. Scaredy-cat though he was, Titus would normally already have been running to join them.

"Titus!"

Still no reaction. Exasperated, Maximus turned on his heels, followed by Aghiles. He stood in front of Titus and looked him up and down. "Well?" He looked down the corridor Titus had just inspected. It was as dark and silent as the others. "You see? There's no one there. No phantom." His tone was sharp, almost mocking.

Cut to the quick, Titus stood up straight. He refused to be spoken to as if he were a coward and a fool. He was sure he had seen something. "If you don't go check," he said, "I'm not budging." He crossed his arms over his chest and stuck out his chin. "And as you don't know the Colosseum…"

Maximus could have strangled him. "Fine," he snapped. "But remind me later to wring your neck!"

They plunged into the corridor.

"The second door," Titus instructed them.

Maximus' step was tense and hurried. When he reached the second door, he flung it open and went into the room. Seconds later, he came back out, as white as a sheet.

"Aghiles! Titus! Come quickly!"

A white figure was laid out on the ground. When the three boys approached, it twitched slightly. Instinctively, Titus hid behind Aghiles. It was a phantom, just as he had said. But his curiosity got the better of him, and he decided to risk a peek. To tell the truth, he had imagined phantoms a bit more vaporous, a bit less physical. This one looked more like an old man in very bad shape. If he hadn't twitched, the three friends would have been convinced they had found a dead body.

The man—because it was indeed a man—was so thin his bones could be seen through his dry, gray skin, withered like parchment. He clearly hadn't eaten for days, or had anything to drink either. He had open sores here and there, covered in dirt. And there were tiny red tooth bites on his legs. The rats had made a feast of him. His face was hidden behind a scruffy gray beard. His ragged clothes stunk of filth, urine, and rotting. He looked like the living dead—because he was, after all, still alive. His huge eyes glowed feverishly out of his sunken face.

Aghiles was the first to crouch down beside the man. "What's your name?" he asked.

The man opened his mouth. He wanted to speak, but no sound came out. Aghiles laid his hand on his thin arm and squeezed it. "We'll get you out of here."

When Maximus overcame his amazement, he tapped his friend on the shoulder and signaled to him to stand up. He pulled him and Titus to one side and said in a hushed voice, "What are you taking about, Aghiles? We can't get him out of here!"

"Why not?"

"Because he's a prisoner! The gods alone know why he's here. But it's certainly not without good reason."

"I don't see what the problem is," said Aghiles.

"The problem? The problem is that we'll be outlaws if we assist a prisoner."

"Are you afraid?"

"Of him? No. Given the state he's in, he can't do much to us."

"So?"

"But I *am* afraid of the law, yes," Maximus continued. "You can get locked up for helping a prisoner. To say nothing of the disgrace it would bring upon my father."

Titus considered. He didn't want to get his friend into trouble. "If you're not willing to take the risk," he said, "maybe we can ask someone else to help. Your father, for example. He could find out who this man is and whether anything can be done for him."

"Would you dare admit we'd broken into the Colosseum illegally?"

Titus frowned. "But you surely don't want to just leave him here?" he asked.

Maximus uncomfortably averted his eyes.

"No! Don't tell me!" Aghiles thundered. "You're not saying we should leave him here? That's beneath you. Could you look yourself in the mirror after that? I couldn't!"

"Let's not let our emotions run away with us," Maximus replied. "It's complicated enough already. Let's consider things coldly, from the legal point of view."

"You're heartless," Titus said.

The words stung Maximus, but if anyone had to keep a cool head, he did. He had to weigh the risk they would run if they helped this man. He had to listen to his head, not his heart. Even if doing so seemed heartless.

Then Aghiles stood up and looked Maximus straight in the eye. "Maximus, I request permission to be left behind. I must help this man, on my own, if necessary. I'll manage somehow. If I'm caught, I risk the death penalty, I know it, since I'm a slave. I accept that. That would have been my fate anyway, if I had landed in the hands of any master other than you."

Maximus began to speak but Aghiles stopped him. "Otherwise, I could never sleep again."

"Me neither," Titus added.

Maximus gave a loud sigh and looked at the suffering figure lying there. He closed his eyes, considered a moment, and then stood up. "Okay," he said, "we'll help him. But on one condition: when he's got his strength back, we'll turn him in to the police. They can decide what to do with him after that."

Titus nodded his agreement.

Aghiles wasn't completely satisfied, but it was better than nothing. "We need to start by finding him some water," he said.

Maximus turned to Titus. "Do you know if there's a well in the Colosseum?"

Titus nodded. "I'm on my way!" He rushed out but stopped short after just a few steps. The silence had suddenly enveloped him. And the shadows too. He hesitated, started going back, but then changed his mind. He raised his hand and petted the little monkey snuggled against his shoulder. The warmth reassured him.

"Come on, Dux! We'll show them we're real men too!" He turned bravely and ventured a little further into the bowels of the Colosseum.

To keep his nerve, he thought about the lively atmosphere that reigned here during the games. The corridors were so narrow, it was almost impossible to get around without bumping into other people. Men would be carrying about planks of scenery or plants, dragging prisoners in chains, carrying food and wine to the gladiators. The air would echo the blows of the hammers working on the weapons. The whole place would be filled with the chatter and the cries of the spectators, along with the roaring of the wild beasts.

The hypogeum, ordinarily so lively and noisy, was the complete opposite now.

At last, at the end of a corridor, Titus found the well he was seeking. He was proud of himself; his memory of the place hadn't let him down. In his mind's eye, he could even recall the way to the hall where his father kept his wild animals before each show. It was at the end of a corridor that opened onto a long series of rooms the workmen used during the games. Ironworkers, woodworkers, potters, cabinetmakers, costume makers, blacksmiths—they all worked, ate, and slept in those compartments.

Titus went to the edge of the well and lowered the bucket. It struck water a few yards down with a splash that echoed. He then pulled it clattering back up to him. When Titus looked at the bucketful of water, he frowned. He had no cup with him. So he took a fold of his tunic and plunged it in the water. Once it was well soaked, he gathered it up and made his way back along the path, trying to cup the dripping water in his hands. Suddenly he heard voices.

"Water duty! Why is it always me on water duty!?"

Titus froze. The voice was coming from the other end of the corridor. It was coming closer. Someone was headed straight for him.

XVII

ALARM!

"Are you sure you heard correctly?" the man asked Flavia.

The woman withheld a sigh of frustration. It was the nth time she had been made to repeat what she had heard and the nth time she had been doubted. She was starting to lose patience. But this time, it was one of their leaders who was questioning her. And she didn't want to seem disrespectful.

"Yes, Caius. It was my brother who told me." She blushed. "He's a soldier," she added, a little ashamed.

If only her brother didn't sometimes have to arrest Christians, Flavia would be infinitely proud of him. Like her, he was the child of a slave. Yet he had become a soldier. In theory, that was impossible. But, when very young, he managed to get himself noticed by a military chief who took him under his wing and helped him up the ladder.

"And did he tell you when?" Caius asked.

Flavia shook her head. "He didn't know. But very soon, he thought."

Caius paced up and down, scratching his chin with a concerned look on his face. The little group of men and women around him were silent. They watched him, worried, ready to carry out his orders. And yet, Caius looked nothing like a leader. Rather small, thin, and in delicate health, he had gentle features and a high-pitched voice. But he was enormously respected. Caius was one of the few priests in this little Christian community hiding in Rome. He was one of the pillars among the most fervent defenders of Christ. He was frail but courageous. And his words carried more weight than anyone else's. He had faith strong enough to move mountains and an immense love for his flock.

"Emperor Diocletian is the devil incarnate," said one man with a sigh. "Until now, he'd at least respected our dead…"

"It's not the dead he's concerned about," Caius explained. "It's what he thinks we're doing with them. Or, rather, what others imagine…" He smiled bleakly. "He takes us for cannibals because we proclaim that the bread we eat in the Eucharist is the Body of our Lord. But, from that, to imagine we eat our dead!"

"But the emperor's an intelligent man! He knows very well that's not true!"

"The emperor, yes; but the people, no. Rumor has spread. People are afraid."

"He's right," agreed Flavia. "People think we're bloodthirsty."

"The emperor wants to reassure the crowds," Caius went on. "If he sends soldiers into the catacombs, he can provide the proof the people are expecting."

"That will say we really are cannibals!" said a woman, taking offense.

Caius sadly nodded his head. "It all depends on what Diocletian decides. If he wants to calm the people down, he'll confirm that the bodies of our dead are safe and sound. But if he wants to stir things up and turn the people against us even more, he only has to tell them we've eaten them."

Flavia shivered. Everyone around her fell into stunned silence.

"In the meantime, we have to warn everyone that the catacombs are no longer safe," Caius continued. He spoke softly, but his voice was perfectly clear and firm.

"No one must hide there anymore! We have to redouble our vigilance. Be wary of any strangers!" He stopped and slowly looked from one to the other. "And avoid any needless violence."

The men and women around him all nodded their heads. Then the priest raised his hand and made the Sign of the Cross over them.

The little group dispersed in silence. No one must know they had been there, especially not the master of the house. The next time, they would gather somewhere else, to cover their tracks.

XVIII

WATER DUTY

Cowering in the shadows, Titus held his breath. He had just slipped into a nook in the wall when a boy balancing a bucket on each arm passed by him. Titus' eyes popped out of his head: it was his thief! No doubt about it. He recognized him. And what's more, he recognized the *bulla* swinging around his neck. His *bulla*! Titus clenched his fists and closed his eyes. If only he were big and strong and courageous—he would jump him, snatch back the amulet, and stick the boy's head in a bucket of water. He would make him give the names of all his accomplices. But, instead, Titus didn't move a muscle. If he were found out, the whole gang would be on top of him like a ton of bricks.

Titus froze at the thought. He felt his legs turn to jelly and feared he was about to collapse. He let go of the wet fold of his tunic and braced his two hands against the wall behind him. His fingers tensed, scratching at the stone, trying to find a hold to support him. In desperate silence, he called on all the gods of Rome: Jupiter, Vulcan, Neptune, Pluto, Diana, Mars, Juno...

Not far from him, near the well, the boy was taking his time, still grumbling. He clearly resented having to do this chore and was in no hurry to get it done.

Titus hardly dared to breathe. His tunic was dripping—plop! plop!—onto his sandals. To him, each drop seemed to make a

81

terrible racket, but he didn't dare move to gather up the wet folds. Fortunately, the sounds of the boy drawing water drowned out the noise he was making.

After what seemed an eternity, Titus at last heard the boy grab his buckets and head back. But hardly a yard away from Titus, he stopped. Titus closed his eyes, fearing the game was up.

But the boy only put down his buckets to wrap a fold of his tunic around each of the metal handles to protect his hands. He trudged past Titus without noticing him.

Titus waited until he could no longer hear the boy before he carefully ventured out of the shadows. But then he gave in to panic and began running as fast as his legs could carry him to the other end of the hypogeum. As he ran, he kicked up the dust around him, his sandals clacking on the ground. But Titus didn't care. He just wanted to get out of there as quickly as possible!

When he at last arrived, he slammed the door behind him, leaned against the wall, and took a deep breath. Maximus and Aghiles jumped and looked at him with alarm. Then, a little smile crept onto Maximus' lips. "You managed, then?" he asked a little sarcastically, assuming Titus had just made a cowardly retreat.

Slowly, very slowly, Titus nodded his head and took a deep gulp. "I saw him," he said at last.

His friends didn't know what he meant.

"I saw him!" When no one reacted, Titus added, "I saw my thief!"

With that, Aghiles jumped to his feet. "Is he following you?"

Titus smiled, reassured to be back among friends. He shook his head. "No, he didn't see me."

"Was he alone?" asked Maximus.

"Yes, he came to fetch water right in front of me."

Suddenly remembering why he had risked his life in the

hypogeum in the first place, Titus felt the bottom of his tunic and found the fold he had dipped in water. "I didn't have a cup," he apologized as he brought the wet cloth to the prisoner's mouth and pressed it against his lips. The prisoner sucked greedily at the bitter water.

When he had finished, Maximus returned to the subject at hand. "You're sure you really saw someone?"

"By Pollux, yes, I swear it!" Titus shouted. "He was on water duty. He went back with two buckets full!"

"And it was your thief?"

"I'd bet my life on it! He was even wearing my *bulla*! Oh, the horrible dog!"

"If he went to draw water," Maximus said, "that means they really are living here, well settled in the Colosseum. You didn't see anyone else?"

Titus shook his head vigorously. "They must be living in the workmen's shops," he added after a moment. "They must have found mattresses there, and braziers to cook on. My father always clears out the place where he keeps the animals, but I know the others leave their things in their workshops."

Maximus could feel his adrenaline rising. He imagined a handful of boys, comfortably settled in the Colosseum, convinced they were invulnerable. What a triumph it would be to catch them unaware! He raised his head and met the gaze of Aghiles. They were both already licking their lips in delight!

A moan brought them both down to earth. The prisoner was in pain. He had opened his mouth once again as if to speak, but no words came out.

"He's hungry," said Aghiles, rushing to his side. "He'll pass out if he doesn't get anything to eat."

"But we don't have anything," insisted Maximus.

Somehow understanding it was a question of food, Dux stretched his hand out under his master's nose.

"Oh, Dux, no! You've already eaten almost all the—"

Titus stopped short; he had an idea. He shoved his hand into his pocket, tapped the little purse where he kept the seeds for his monkey, and pulled out a few. Dux wriggled on his master's shoulder at the sight of this feast, but Titus offered them to the man lying on the ground.

"I'm afraid that's all I have," he said. "My monkey has eaten all the rest. But this should keep you going."

The man gave him a weak smile and slowly put his hand out for this blessed food. But Dux didn't see things the same way. He jumped on Titus' shoulder, grabbing two seeds on the way.

"Dux! Give that back!"

As fast as lightning, the little animal stuck the seeds in his mouth. Titus went red with frustration.

"I'm so sorry," he stammered. "I'm trying to train him…"

After eating just a dozen or so seeds, the man stopped. His stomach was complaining. The water he had drunk was already giving him stabbing pains.

What crime could this man have committed to deserve such treatment? the boys wondered. Even the worst killer deserved better! A quick death in the arena was surely less punishment than to die of hunger and thirst.

Aghiles looked for a long moment at the prisoner before turning to his friends. "I think we first must care for this man. We can deal with the den of thieves later."

XIX

RESCUE

Blandula gave a start. Someone had just knocked on the door. She looked around her and saw the starry sky above her head. She had fallen asleep on the patio. And now there was that knocking again. The girl scampered to a corner and held her breath. She was terrified. They had come for her!

Unconsciously, Blandula had been waiting for this moment ever since her master had been arrested. She was only astonished it had taken them this long. Under torture, Master Cornelius would surely have given her name. He would also have confessed about the forbidden book she had found in the old man's bedroom. Blandula should have gotten rid of that book—burned it or thrown it out. She knew it could only lead to her downfall. And yet, she couldn't. Master Cornelius was so attached to it. He was an intelligent man, brilliant even. He wouldn't have loved that book so much for no reason. She had put it away in the chest in his bedroom.

The banging on the door grew louder, more insistent. Blandula was surprised no one was yelling, ordering her to open the door. That was normally what the guards did. And then she suddenly realized that the knocking wasn't coming from the front door, but from the door leading out to the lane behind the villa. What if someone had at last come to tell her where they had taken her master's body? Who would come at night at the risk of his life to pass on the information? The girl hesitated. She trembled. Slowly, she crept out of her corner.

More knocking. What if the person went away before she had time to open up? Blandula hurried; she ran to the door.

"I'm coming!" she shouted as she threw the door wide open. Aghiles jumped.

"Oh! It's you!" Blandula sounded disappointed. Aghiles shuffled his feet awkwardly. He didn't know what to say. When he had finally made up his mind to come here, he hadn't thought this far ahead. But fortunately, Maximus emerged from the shadows toward the girl. She looked at him in fright, took a step back, and started to close the door.

"No! Please! Wait!" It was Aghiles who spoke. "Maximus is my friend. My master."

"So, nothing happened to him then," thought Blandula, recalling Aghiles' worry and his hurry to leave when she wanted to dress his wounds. "At least he's safe and sound."

But Maximus was in a pitiful state. His face was haggard, his hair tousled, and his tunic crumpled and dirty. Above all, he looked tense. He kept looking behind him to the end of the lane. "We need your help," he hurriedly whispered. "Aghiles told us what you did for him. You're our only chance."

"Please…," the voice of Titus came out of the shadows by the side of the house.

Blandula instinctively leaned out to see who it was. She froze.

She took a quick step back and looked at Aghiles, not understanding. He gave her a weak, embarrassed smile. "We didn't know where else to go…"

"It will soon be daybreak," added Maximus. "If anyone spots us, we're done for!"

After hesitating a moment, Blandula finally opened the door to them. It was completely instinctive and totally unwise, but she somehow had the feeling it was what Master Cornelius would want her to do.

Without losing a second, Aghiles rushed to Titus in the shadows. He knelt down, gripped a nearly lifeless body under the arms, and lifted him onto his shoulder. He stood and carried his fragile cargo into the villa. Maximus and Titus followed right behind. After checking again that no one had seen them, they closed the door behind them.

When the three friends were at last safe inside, they breathed more easily. They had thought they would never get there. The way back through the sewers of the Colosseum had been long and difficult. And, when they came back out onto the street and realized that the city was slowly awakening, a cold sweat of panic overcame them. Maximus was very worried. It had been no use reassuring him that the house where Aghiles had found refuge earlier that evening wasn't far. They still weren't sure they would make it there before dawn. And they weren't sure that Blandula would even open the door to them.

"It's a prisoner," Maximus whispered, thinking it best to be honest right from the start. "We found him in one of the Colosseum cells. We don't know who he is, but we couldn't leave him there in this state."

If the information surprised the girl, she didn't let it show. Without a word, she led them through the villa to a small, sparsely decorated room. There was nothing but a little toilet stand sitting on a tiny table near the window. This was clearly her room. Blandula pointed Aghiles to the bed. He hesitated. The prisoner was so filthy.

"Don't worry," Blandula reassured him, as though reading his thoughts.

Aghiles again knelt and laid the man on the bed. Against the clean sheets, his pitiful state stood out even more.

Blandula approached and, overcoming her revulsion, took a good long look at him. He smelled, he was dirty, and he was covered with sores. He didn't move. His eyes were closed. He was frighteningly pale.

"Is he dead?" she asked.

The three boys looked at her in a daze. Their muscles were aching. They were ready to drop from exhaustion. The climb out of the sewers had sapped all their strength. Especially Aghiles. He had dug deep into his last reserves of energy to carry the man this far.

"He passed out," Maximus explained, his voice cracking from thirst.

A few hours earlier, when Aghiles had first hoisted the man onto his shoulder, to his horror, he had seemed light as a feather. But once the man had passed out, he seemed as heavy as a boulder. His body was like a dead weight. They had inched forward, crouched down, their lungs struggling for air in the stench of the sewer and the man's clothing. For Aghiles, it had been torture shuffling ahead bent over.

Blandula reached her hand toward the wounded man to take his pulse. It was weak, but it was there. She raised her head and smiled at them. "He's alive!"

Then, without a word, she left the room and came back with clean cloths. Then she disappeared again for a bit longer and came back with a basin and a steaming jug of water.

The three boys watched her work, incapable of shaking off their overwhelming fatigue. It was only when she turned to them and suggested that they go wash at the fountain in the patio that they snapped out of it.

"It's the best I can suggest at the moment," she said with a smile. "Go freshen up; I'll take care of him."

When Aghiles, Maximus, and Titus returned to the bedroom a little while later, Blandula had washed the man from head to foot to remove the stench of his oozing sores. She had dressed his wounds and anointed them with soothing oils and balms. She had shaved his beard and covered him in a clean sheet. She was used to this. Master Cornelius hadn't been in the prime of life; it was she who had cared for him, had helped him to dress and to shave.

The man's eyes were still closed, but he was now breathing easily. In the light of the lamp Blandula had placed next to him, he looked much less old. He looked more like a young man who must have had a strong constitution before his arrest. That would explain how he could have survived in such conditions. Anyone weaker wouldn't have held out for long.

Blandula looked at him for a long moment with a sad smile on her lips. "He must have seen my master just before his death," she murmured with tears in her eyes.

"Your master?" Maximus asked her.

Blandula sniffled and looked at the boys. "My master, Cornelius. The soldiers took him away a few days ago. He was a Christian, and I know they killed him in the Colosseum at the last games."

Maximus looked at his friends, who had just had the same thought: The man they rescued is a Christian?! That was all they needed!

XX

A PANG OF CONSCIENCE

"A Christian!" Titus shouted when the three friends were again alone.

Blandula had gone to prepare something for them to eat, for they hadn't had anything since lunch the day before. Their stomachs were grumbling loudly. They were starving.

Maximus pursed his lips, then said, "That's just our luck! The most sought-after enemy in the whole Roman Empire. If we're caught, it won't just be prison: it'll be death..."

"Well, then, we'll just have to be even more careful," Aghiles said simply.

Titus and Maximus were aghast.

"That's all you've got to say?" exclaimed Titus.

"About what?"

"That he's a Christian!"

Aghiles shrugged his shoulders. "I don't see how that changes our plans."

"If I'd known that..." Titus grumbled.

Now it was Aghiles' turn to be aghast. "Hold on, hold on," he said. "And if this man had killed his whole family and his neighbors? Would you still have helped him?"

"That's not the same."

"Not the same!"

"Aghiles," said Maximus, trying to calm him down.

"I'm sorry, Maximus, but I need to understand. What crime did this man commit?"

"He doesn't believe in the same gods we do!" said Titus.

Aghiles broke out in a nervous laugh. "But I don't believe in them either!"

"Aghiles, shush! You'll wake him up."

Aghiles stretched his arm toward the man and said, "Explain to me why he deserves to die."

"Aghiles!" This time Maximus' tone was stern, like that of a master giving his slave an order. "It's more complicated than that," he went on in a calmer voice. "You have to understand that Christians are bloodthirsty barbarians."

"Him? A bloodthirsty barbarian?"

"They're cannibals!"

"Cannibals?!"

Maximus felt a little awkward. "Well…that's what I've heard. Whenever they meet, they eat human flesh and drink blood."

Aghiles looked at him in disbelief. He was about to say something but held his tongue. Maximus was his master. He didn't have the right to argue with him. That didn't stop him from thinking it, and the look on his face was enough to make Maximus very ill at ease. For Maximus knew what his friend was thinking, and, in all honesty, he knew he was right. Maximus didn't put much stock in his religion, its gods, and its superstitions. He often even made fun of it. Yet about this new religion, this Christianity, he seemed ready to believe anything, even the most outrageous things.

"In any case, Christian or not, that has nothing to do with our plans," Maximus at last said to calm things down. "Once he's back on his feet, we'll hand him over to the authorities. We'll find some plausible explanation."

"But he'll talk," Titus said. "He could denounce us under torture."

"That's why we have to avoid giving away too much about ourselves. And he must not leave here for any reason whatsoever."

"What were you talking about?"

Blandula's ringing voice made them jump. They turned to her, embarrassed, and saw she was carrying an armful of dishes. Each of the boys grabbed one. They were so hungry!

"I did the best with what I could find," Blandula said. "My master's food reserves are starting to dwindle." The girl also had a scroll tucked under her arm.

"Is that for us too?" Maximus asked her, pointing to the object.

Blandula blushed and shook her head. "N…no," she stammered. "It's for your prisoner."

"What is it?"

She looked at Maximus with a touch of worry, but then handed him the book she had fetched from her master's room.

"It belonged to Master Cornelius. I thought your man here might like it. He no doubt needs some comfort after all he's been through."

The three boys looked at one another out of the corner of their eyes. Hearing her speak with such concern about this man, they were ashamed of the conversation they had just been having. She hadn't asked any questions, as they had. She had simply taken in the poor man. More than that, she had even accepted the danger that came with him. If there were denouncements, Titus, Maximus, and Aghiles could escape by denying any knowledge of this house; Blandula couldn't.

Maximus turned the scroll over in his hands. It didn't take any explaining to know what this book was. He had heard about the Gospels. The emperor had ordered that they be destroyed. People thought them a threat to the whole empire. Yet it looked the same as any other book.

"Have you read it?" he asked.

An embarrassed smile lit up Blandula's face. "Me?"

"Yes."

"Oh, no," she said with a giggle. "I can't read!"

Maximus unrolled the scroll a little and read out a passage at random:

> Then the King will say to those at his right hand, "Come, O blessed of my Father, inherit the kingdom prepared for you from the foundation of the world; for I was hungry and you gave me food, I was thirsty and you gave me drink, I was a stranger and you welcomed me, I was naked and you clothed me, I was sick and you visited me, I was in prison and you came to me."
>
> Then the righteous will answer him, "Lord, when did we see you hungry and feed you, or thirsty and give you drink? And when did we see you a stranger and welcome you, or naked and clothe you? And when did we see you sick or in prison and visit you?"
>
> And the King will answer them, "Truly, I say to you, as you did it to one of the least of these my brethren, you did it to me."[1]

With that, Maximus closed the book, looking troubled.

---

1. Matthew 25:34-40, RSV, 2CE

XXI

PAULUS

The prisoner at last opened his eyes but immediately closed them again. The room was bright, and he wasn't used to the light. He had been shut up for so long. He slowly raised his eyelids again and stared at the ceiling above him. It was white, immaculate. Just like the walls of the room. Could he at last be in paradise, as Christ had promised them?

Suddenly, a slight noise made his heart skip a beat. He tried to raise his head, but he hadn't the strength. He fell heavily back onto the bed. Then the noise came closer. Something appeared in his field of vision.

"An angel!" he thought.

The dark-haired girl smiled and leaned over him.

"How are you feeling?"

The man thought for a moment. Yes, how *was* he feeling? His body felt so light, so ethereal. He opened his mouth to reply, but the words wouldn't come out.

"My name is Blandula. Three boys brought you here. You were in the Colosseum. Do you remember?"

A terrible image flashed through his eyes. His friends. Were they all dead?

Seeing his frightened look, Blandula reassured him. "You're safe here. Would you like to eat something?"

What a silly question! Do people still go on eating in heaven? And yet the shooting pains in his stomach told him the answer. He nodded his head.

The girl gently took him in her arms and raised him up in the bed. Now he could take in the whole room. It was narrow and sparse but very clean and bright. Blandula picked up the tray she had set on the floor. She raised the cover of a bowl, and the delicious aroma of soup filled the room. The man closed his eyes and sniffed the fragrance with delight. He suddenly felt alive and still in this world after all.

Blandula was holding a bowl before her. The man tried to take it, but he was still too weak to hold it. His arms looked like two long sticks of skin and bone. He closed his eyes. Everything was coming back to him. His friends. The soldiers. The cries. The pain. The sneers of the guards. Their savagery. And then, suddenly, nothing. The silence. The cold. The darkness. The solitude. The suffering. The rats. The hunger and thirst. Death, crouching in the shadows, just waiting for its moment.

"Here, let me help you." Blandula sat down next to him and firmly slid the bowl to his lips.

The first gulp burned his tongue, but the next was divine. He drank greedily, with huge slurping noises.

Blandula laughed. "Not too fast! You'll make yourself sick!" She took the bowl away and set it down. "I'll give you more in a little bit. First, what's your name?"

He again opened his mouth to speak, but with no success. So, with his finger, he traced an invisible letter P on the sheet, and then an A, a U, an L, a U, and an S.

Blandula sadly shook her head. "I don't know how to read."

The man raised his feeble hand and silently smiled at her.

"I'll go get the ones who brought you here," Blandula said as

96

she rose. "I know at least one of them knows how to read! Then you'll be able to tell us."

Before going, she looked at the stranger, hesitated, and then said, "My master's name was Cornelius. He was a Christian."

The man stared at her, perking up his ears.

"He was arrested a few days ago. They told me he was fed to the lions." She shivered. The man was now staring at her so hard, she continued in a whisper, "Did you know him?"

The man very slightly bowed his head in a yes.

"Did you see him?"

The same slight nod of the head.

Blandula's eyes filled with tears. "So you know where they've taken him!" she exclaimed in a broken voice. "I so want to make sure he's been given a dignified burial."

The stranger closed his eyes. Yes, he knew…

The arrival of the three boys gave him a start. Maximus, Titus, and Aghiles burst in when they heard Blandula speaking to him.

She immediately turned to them. "He's doing much better! He tried to tell me his name, but I can't read," she said with a blush. "And he knows where my master is as well."

Maximus stiffened. "Your master? But you told us he was dead."

"Yes, but I don't know where they've buried him, and for several days now, I haven't been able to sleep not knowing where to find him. I want to be sure he's been given a decent tomb."

Maximus turned to the man, still sitting on the bed propped up on the pillows. "Do you know where to find the body of her master?" he asked.

The man blinked his eyes several times.

Maximus took a long look at him. In silence. He wasn't sure how he should behave with him. As long as he had been lifeless and looking like a corpse, it had been easy to keep his distance. But now… "What's your name?" he at last asked him.

The man again began tracing letters on the sheet as he had done for Blandula. Maximus went closer and read them out.

"P-A-U-L-U-S," he read. "Paulus. Your name is Paulus?"

The man smiled.

"Paulus!" exclaimed Titus. "That's great! My name is Titus! And this is Aghiles and Maximus." He stuck out his chest with an air of importance, proud to be the one making the introductions. "We're the ones who saved—"

Titus stopped short. Maximus had just shot him a furious, withering look.

XXII

A SHADOW IN THE NIGHT

Maximus opened his eyes and looked around him. Everything was in darkness. It was night. He must have slept much longer than he thought.

Blandula had sent the boys home in the middle of the morning, insisting that they get some rest. Maximus, Aghiles, and Titus at first protested that they weren't tired. But then they looked from one to the other and burst out laughing. Despite their quick wash at the fountain in the patio and the welcome meal Blandula had prepared them, they looked terrible. They had dark rings under their feverish eyes, and their tunics were torn and dirty. And Titus still bore the marks from the attack the day before.

"I'll take care of Paulus," Blandula had said. "He too surely needs to sleep."

Sleep? Maximus was sure he would never fall asleep with so many things running around in his mind. And yet, his head hardly hit the pillow when he fell into a deep, dreamless sleep. And he slept straight through from noon till the middle of the night.

Maximus folded his arms behind his head, stared at the ceiling of his bedroom, and considered. He must work out a plan of action. He frowned. What an idiot, that Titus! He never knew when to keep quiet. Now, Paulus knew all of their names.

For the moment, the man still couldn't speak, but it was only a question of time. And then he would be able to tell everything that had happened. With a little luck, no one would believe what he said. Christians were considered liars and schemers. But it would only take one soldier a little more curious than the others, and more tough, and that would be that. It wouldn't be hard to track down the three boys. Not that Titus and Maximus were unusual names, but two boys in the company of a tall black slave and a little monkey—you didn't come across that every day. Even in Rome.

"We've got to get him away from here," thought Maximus. "Get him to a town where no one can link him to us. Not unless they carried out a really thorough search."

But it remained to be seen how they could get Paulus out of the city without being caught.

Maximus turned the question over in his mind, until he heard a little noise outside his window. He squinted his eyes and searched the half-light. Nothing. He must have dreamed it. Suddenly, a figure loomed up at the window. Maximus didn't even have time to shout before the figure was upon him, straddling him to keep him still. Then he clapped his hand so violently over Maximus' mouth that Maximus felt he was crushing his windpipe. He shook his head from side to side, trying to get free. But the man only pressed his hand down harder. Maximus was suffocating, kicking his feet and twisting about. He tried to drag his attacker onto the floor. But the man had his full weight on him. With his free hand, the man grabbed a cushion and held it over Maximus' face. Then he leaned to his ear and threateningly murmured, "If you tell what you saw in the Colosseum, the next time, I'll kill you! You and your friends too!"

Then, just as suddenly as the man had arrived, he stood up and left through the window in one bound. Maximus pulled the cushion away from his face, opened his mouth, and breathed like a drowning man coming up for air. Then he felt his chest, making sure he hadn't any broken ribs, and sat up on the edge of his bed. It was useless trying to go after the attacker; he was long gone. His heart was beating wildly. His neck was soaked in a cold sweat. He hadn't seen anything, understood anything. It was all so quick. He had no idea who this man could have been. Perhaps a friend of Paulus?

XXIII

HESITATION

Aghiles looked at his friend out of the corner of his eye. He had seemed strange ever since they left the house. He was tense. Jumpy. He kept looking behind him at the passersby. Gave a start when anyone bumped into him. And at this time of day, that was inevitable. He was nervously scanning everything around him.

"Maximus, are you all right?" he asked.

"Yeah, yeah. I didn't sleep well."

It was a half-truth, because during the second half of the night, he hadn't closed an eyelid.

"Are you worried about something?"

Maximus hadn't told Aghiles anything about the intruder. He was afraid of how his friend would react. Aghiles was hotheaded, capable of lashing out at the first comer. But that was just the problem: Maximus didn't know who had threatened him. On reflection, he no longer thought it was a Christian who had attacked him. That just didn't make sense. These days, who would dare boast about having saved a Christian? No one. And above all, not Maximus. And then, if the Christians knew that Paulus had been left behind in the Colosseum, they surely would have gotten to him first. Perhaps the thief of Titus' *bulla*? Or one of his accomplices? If that were the case, it was proof they had gotten involved in something important—and dangerous.

Maximus shivered and then looked up at his friend and smiled. No, he wouldn't say anything just yet. He needed to think about it all a bit longer. In any case, this was no time to get distracted. There was Paulus to deal with; they had to find a way to get him off their hands. That was the most urgent problem. "I'm worried about our involvement with Paulus," he said. "I can't wait till we have nothing more to do with him. It's all too risky."

While he was speaking, he noticed a boy standing to one side, his back against a wall, staring at him. He didn't try to hide it. On the contrary, he even seemed to flaunt his cocky attitude, with a little smirk on his lips. Maximus looked away. And when he looked back over his shoulder, the boy had disappeared. Maximus must have imagined him.

XXIV

HOPES

A few minutes later, when Maximus, Titus, and Aghiles met up again at Blandula's, she opened the door to them right away.

"He spoke!" she announced, beaming.

Maximus shot a quick look back at the street and went into the house. Hoping to pass as ordinary visitors, they had gone in by the front door. But that was no reason to draw attention to themselves. At this time of day, the street was very busy.

"Are you mad?" he hissed at her once the door was shut. "The whole street can hear you!"

Blandula went pale. "Sorry…," she stammered. "I wasn't paying attention."

That's just what Maximus was worried about. If Blandula wasn't careful, they ran an even a greater risk. The situation was growing more and more urgent. They couldn't afford to waste any more time like this.

"He spoke?" he asked after a moment.

Blandula nodded and smiled. "I went to see him this morning with a bowl of hot broth. And when he'd drunk it, he thanked me."

"So he's feeling better?"

The girl frowned. "Well, he spoke, but he's still very weak. He still can't get up."

Maximus scowled.

"But in the meantime, he told me where I can find my master! All of the martyred Christians are buried in the catacombs outside the gates of the city."

"The catacombs? But there are several of them."

"I know, but Paulus told me the one where Cornelius is likely to be." Blandula flushed, hesitated, and then dared to ask, "Would one of you agree to go there with me? I'd like to pay my last respects to my master, but I'm afraid to go on my own."

Titus awkwardly stared at his feet. In the public mind, these burial places were filled with spirits and ghosts of every kind. He perfectly understood Blandula's fears, but he lacked the courage to go. Besides, the risk of discovery was too great.

"I'll go," said Aghiles. "Whenever you're ready." He turned to Maximus and asked, "Do I have your permission?"

After quick reflection, Maximus nodded his head. "But, above all, be careful," he said. "This isn't the time to get caught."

Aghiles smiled. "You heard what Blandula said: the catacombs are sort of neutral territory."

Maximus frowned. If only he could believe it. "We'll take care of Paulus," he said. "Titus and I will deal with him."

Aghiles shot him a long and slightly suspicious look. Maximus decided to let it pass. It suited him to have Aghiles and Blandula out of the way. They wouldn't disturb his bad conscience. Maximus had no intention of betraying his friend, but he wanted to deal with things as quickly, as simply, and above all as safely as possible. And to do that, he needed to take a step back. To keep his distance and a cool head—that's what was needed. There was no room for sentiment.

XXV

A TRUE TREASURE

Fulgur put his sack full of gold pieces back in its hiding place and laid the stone back in its place. He kicked a bit of dirt over it with the tip of his toe. Another few sacksful like that, and it would all be over. Goodbye, Rome! Goodbye, cursed city! Just a little more time and Fulgur would have amassed enough money to buy a boat and sail far away. Very far. Egypt, probably. Or some other country where no one knew him and no one would be searching for him. Where he wouldn't have to live in hiding anymore. Where he could spend his wealth openly. Fulgur had been waiting for this moment for so long. He wasn't going to let three kids and a monkey get in his way. He wouldn't let them spoil everything now.

There was a knock at the door.
"Yes?"
A young boy entered the room, his head slightly bowed.
"The slave, the giant, he's gone out, Fulgur."
"The slave?"
"Yes."
"Was he alone?"
"No, there was a girl with him."

Fulgur thought a moment. No one would ever listen to a slave, whatever he said. His word was worthless. Even if he was incredibly strong, he wasn't the danger.

"We're having him followed, though," the boy added.

"And the two others?"

"They're still inside the house. We're keeping a close eye on it. At the front and the back. Someone's watching Senator Julius Claudius' house too. Just in case."

Fulgur nodded his head. "Good, keep it up! I need to know every move they make."

"Yes, Fulgur." The boy hesitated before daring to add, "But I don't think the senator's son will talk. He's too scared."

Fulgur furrowed his brow and exploded, "Who asked for your opinion!?"

A spark of fright lit the boy's eyes. "No…no…no one, Fulgur. I was just saying—"

"Well, don't say anything, and just carry out my orders."

"Of course, of course, Fulgur."

"Now get out of here!" His tone of voice left no room for argument. "Get out and let me know their every movement!"

The boy didn't need to be told twice. He scurried from the room on the double.

"Stupid idiot!" growled Fulgur with a sneer.

By Jupiter, how he hated all these boys hanging onto him like a bunch of leeches! If he didn't need them to make his fortune, he would have gotten rid of them long ago. And to think some of them thought of him as a big brother or a father. Ha! Fulgur spat on the ground. All that sissy stuff made him sick!

XXVI

AN OLD CARETAKER

Near the outskirts of the city, Blandula and Aghiles arrived at a vast field full of dozens of tombs. Some of them were already very old. New burials now took place in the underground tunnels dug out to make best use of the limited patch of land.

Blandula had expected to find the same desolate atmosphere as in the other burial sites that surrounded the city, where bodies were burned day and night, making the air unbreathable. But here, there wasn't a bonfire in sight. No nauseating stench. What's more, the place was deserted.

"Are you sure it's here?" she asked Aghiles.

He carefully scoured the landscape and spotted an old man sitting on a rock. He looked toward them. Aghiles gave him a little nod, but the old man didn't move.

"Let's go ask that man," he said. "Maybe he'll be able to tell us."

The two walked toward him. As they approached, the old man slowly turned his head to them. Aghiles bowed slightly, and Blandula smiled in greeting. But the man still gave no reaction. He kept his head slightly bent to the side as though he were listening to something. After a moment, he at last asked, "Who's there?" He stretched out a trembling hand, feeling about him in the empty air.

"He's blind," whispered Aghiles.

The old man suddenly rose and smiled, revealing the few teeth that remained to him. "Yes, I'm blind," he said, "but I'm not deaf! Where are your manners? Has no one ever taught you to introduce yourself properly, young man? Who are you?"

"We've come from Rome," Aghiles replied.

"I knew that already, my boy. I heard you coming from the north."

The two young people looked at each other in amazement.

"I can even tell there are two of you. You don't have the same gait. One of you must be a lot taller than the other."

Blandula instinctively turned and looked up at Aghiles. She smiled for it was true: the Numidian was enormously tall.

"Am I wrong?"

"Uhh, no," stammered Aghiles, ill at ease.

The old man gave an even bigger smile, delighted that he had impressed them. He always liked to show off his powers of perception. Aghiles looked him over a little suspiciously. You could never be too careful. He hadn't let his guard down for an instant since they had left the house.

"And stop looking at me like that," the old man added. "My eyes are truly blind; they've never seen the light of day." To prove his words, he proudly raised his head and turned it from side to side to show them his eyes, which were both milky and clouded over.

"My name is Augustus, and I'm the caretaker of this ceme-tery," he said. "Can I be of assistance?"

Aghiles was about to speak, but Blandula beat him to it, saying, "Greetings to you, Augustus! My name is Blandula."

The old man's face suddenly lit up. "Ah, a young woman! Now, that, I hadn't guessed."

Blandula gave an amused little smile and leaned down to him.

"I'm looking for my master, Cornelius. I know he's here somewhere."

"There's no one here but me."

"Cornelius died."

The caretaker's face darkened.

"Last week, in the Colosseum," Blandula continued, in a faltering voice.

"May his soul rest in peace," the old man murmured.

"I need to know where he is so I can be sure he had a decent burial."

"You loved him, then?" asked the old man.

"He was a good man."

The caretaker tilted his head to one side, as though he were carefully observing the young woman, looking into her heart. Blandula blushed, suddenly feeling awkward. She wasn't used to blind people. Especially this one who, despite his handicap, seemed to be able to read her so clearly.

"What makes you think he's here?" the old man finally asked.

"Aren't all Christians buried in the catacombs?" asked Blandula, troubled.

The man pursed his lips. "He could be somewhere else. Why did you come to this place in particular?"

Blandula didn't know what to say. At a loss, she looked toward Aghiles. He shook his head as if to tell her to watch what she said.

"I…uhh…I just assumed he'd be here."

The man rose. Blandula's hesitation hadn't escaped him.

"If your master was among those who died in the name of Christ, he would have been buried with dignity. Here or elsewhere. The brothers will have looked after his tomb."

"Can I see him?" Blandula asked hopefully.

111

"Who?"

"My master. I'd like to see where he lies."

"There's no point!"

"But…"

"He was given a decent burial, I tell you! Isn't that enough for you?"

"But I need to…"

"You don't trust me, then?"

"It's not that," Blandula stammered. "But the last time I saw Cornelius, he was alive. I can't get used to the idea that he's dead. He was all I had…" The girl stopped, on the verge of tears. "I don't know what to do anymore."

Blandula did indeed feel lost. As long as she had been Cornelius' slave, she had no worries about her future. Her master was a good man; he had always looked after her. When he had freed her, she had chosen to stay by his side. And life still seemed simple to her. But now that he had gone, she was at a loss. She didn't know what would become of her, what she should do. And this strange man frightened her.

The blind man stuck out his chin. "And you?" he asked Aghiles.

"I'm escorting her, that's all."

The caretaker was silent for a moment, considered, and then reached out his hand. "Help me up."

Aghiles stepped forward. The blind man took his arm and stood. With a few subtle but careful touches, he took the measure of the young man before him. Yes, he could tell Aghiles was a veritable force of nature.

"Come," he then said.

The old man grasped a long staff that he used as a cane. He headed toward a corner of the cemetery. Blandula hesitated, but Aghiles gave her a silent nod to follow. She needn't be

112

afraid; he would look after her. The giant Numidian kept an eye on the blind man, watching every one of his moves. But the man didn't give anything away: his face remained blank as he advanced slowly but with an assured step. After winding their way between the tombs, at last the trio stopped. Without even noticing, they had crossed almost the whole of the cemetery and found themselves at a spot in a slight dip in the terrain, hidden from the eyes of those passing by on the road. Before them was the entrance to an underground gallery.

"It's here!" said the caretaker, and he turned and listened for any suspicious noises before entering into the narrow passageway. "Be quick," he whispered. "We mustn't be spotted."

XXVII

WITNESS

When Paulus finally opened his eyes again, he gave a start. Two of the boys who had saved his life were standing by his bedside. They looked to be teenagers. They were talking in lowered voices.

"Good morning," he murmured.

Titus and Maximus immediately fell silent and turned to him. Paulus sensed a certain unease in their eyes.

"Good morning," he repeated.

"Hello," replied Maximus. His tone was cold and distant, far from the warmth of the young woman of the house who had taken care of him till then. Paulus shivered and turned his head to the second boy, the one with a little monkey perched on his shoulder. "Hello . . . Titus, is it?"

Titus bit his lip and frowned. Paulus sensed the tension in the air.

"Is something wrong?" he asked after a long silence. "Isn't Blandula here?"

Maximus shook his head. "She's gone to the catacombs with our friend."

"Gone? Why didn't she tell me she was thinking of going so quickly? I didn't have the chance to tell her how to get in."

"Blandula is a big girl," Maximus snapped. "She didn't think it necessary to ask your permission."

"It's not what you think. You need a password to get into the catacombs."

"A password? But why didn't you say so before?"

"I didn't know she would be going there so soon."

Maximus gave a furious kick against the bedstead. Paulus remained silent. After a long moment, he asked, "You don't like me, do you?"

That startled Maximus. Paulus' frankness threw him. He gathered himself and, after a few seconds, replied in the same level tone of voice. "I've got nothing against you. But I didn't ask for all this. It's far too risky. If it had been up to me, I would have left you in your cell." Maximus wasn't particularly proud of what he just said, but, after all, it was only the truth.

Totally unexpectedly, Paulus smiled. "I understand," he said.

Maximus was taken aback. "You understand?"

"It would have been so easy for you to leave me there. And no one would have ever known. While as now…" He stopped for a moment, and then went on. "Thank you. In these days, it was brave of you to help a Christian."

"Brave? You can say that again! It was sheer madness!"

"My thanks; without you I'd be dead by now." When Titus and Maximus made no reply, Paulus continued, "Twice I should have died, and twice I have been saved. The Lord is great!"

Titus raised his eyebrows. His curiosity got the better of him. "Twice?"

Paulus nodded his head. "I should have met the same fate as my Christian brothers and died in the arena. Instead, I was left huddled in my cell."

"That's not like them," Titus couldn't help observing.

The men who ran the circus games were known for their heartlessness and cruelty. Titus knew them only too well. His

116

father dealt with them often. They were among his best customers. They would go to him to book the wild animals for the spectacles and always reserved the most ferocious. They liked the games to be bloody, to draw roars of horror from the crowd. And what's more, Titus agreed with them. He had been brought up surrounded by the violence of these spectacles, and nothing shocked him anymore. He was always disappointed when the crowd clamored for a victim to be spared.

Paulus looked hard at the boy by his side, trying to read his heart. He wasn't sure what to make of his remark. He nevertheless went on: "When they came to get me, I was at home, in bed. I don't remember it very well. I was delirious with a fever. I had hardly eaten anything for several days. I think the soldiers arrived in the middle of the day. Usually, they come at night, or in the small hours, to be sure they'll find you at home. But that wasn't my case. They must have been tipped off, must have known I'd be there."

Paulus' voice was strangely calm. He wasn't trying to complain. He was just stating the facts, as though the simple facts could mask the horror of it all.

"When they took me away, I could hardly stand up. I seem to recall their fury. Two men had to carry me since I couldn't walk on my own. When they threw me in the—"

"There's no need to tell us all that now. You'll tire yourself again," Maximus interrupted him.

In reality, Maximus couldn't care less how tired Paulus was. He simply didn't want to know his story. The less he knew, the easier it would be to hand him over to the authorities. He must absolutely remain neutral, detached.

"I don't think I would have made much sport for the spectators anyway," Paulus concluded. "I was too weak. That's no doubt why they left me in the cells. In any case, by just forgetting about me, they knew I'd die there anyway." He stopped and gently laid his head back down on the pillow with closed eyes. He still felt so tired. "But if the Lord decided to save me, he must have had other plans for me," he added.

With astonishment, Titus thought he could almost detect a note of regret in his voice. "You're not afraid of dying, then?" he asked with curiosity.

Maximus wrinkled his brow and shot him a dark look.

"Afraid?" asked Paulus. "Everyone's afraid of dying!"

Titus shook his head. "Not you, you Christians. Some of you even smile when faced with the lions. People think you're all mad."

Paulus smiled. "No. It's not death itself that frightens us. It's the suffering. No one wants to suffer. But the promise of the happiness that awaits us is so great, it helps us to overcome our fear of suffering."

"The promise? What promise?"

Paulus turned his head slightly and nodded toward the scroll lying near him. "Have a look at it," he said. "Please, open that book and give it to me."

Titus was about to pick it up when the voice of Maximus stopped him. "Don't, Titus!"

Titus raised his eyes to his friend in surprise. Paulus too looked at Maximus with unmasked surprise. Maximus narrowed his eyes, a little embarrassed, and finally shrugged his shoulders. What good, after all, to make a fuss now, at this point?

Titus grabbed the book and handed it to Paulus, who slowly unrolled it. He was gradually getting his strength back but was still very weak; every gesture required a great effort. After a long moment, he finally found what he was looking for. Then in a voice of renewed force, he read: "Blessed are you when men revile you and persecute you and utter all kinds of evil against you falsely on my account. Rejoice and be glad, for your reward is great in heaven."[1]

Titus said nothing at first. But after a few seconds, he asked, "What reward? A treasure?"

Paulus smiled. "Our reward will be eternal life close to our God."

Maximus smiled mockingly. "Oh, yeah, right!"

Titus looked disappointed. "And that's it?! That's your promised reward?"

Paulus nodded.

Titus gave a skeptical frown. Well, in that case, these Christians really were a little mad. He had hoped they had some miracle recipe to reach eternal happiness, some miracle prayer to recite—he would have been happy to do that—or some offering to make, some new magical amulet...

"It is the promise of being loved forever and unconditionally."

"Yeahhh...," said Titus doubtfully.

"You're suicidal then?" Maximus asked coldly.

"No, none of us seeks death. We just accept it when we have no other choice and place our lives in the hands of the Lord. But, before then, we do what we can to remain alive. We hide, we stay out of sight, we battle on."

"If you value your lives, all you have to do is renounce your religion."

"True, true. But that would also mean renouncing that infinite love..."

---

1. Matthew 5:11-12.

XXVIII

THE CATACOMBS

When Blandula and Aghiles arrived at the bottom of the stairway in the catacombs, they instinctively halted. There was deep silence, total darkness. Aghiles stood up straight, his senses on the alert for the slightest noise. Should they keep going, or should they turn back while there was still time? And what if, beneath his kindly exterior, this caretaker was setting a trap for them?

The old man, still moving forward, suddenly stopped, aware they were no longer following. "What is it? Come on, both of you, follow me."

"It's just that…," Blandula ventured, "we can't see anything."

The caretaker's laugh sounded out of place in these shadows. "What a fool I am!"

He turned, felt along the walls, and grabbed one of the torches the two young people hadn't noticed. As he lit it, the blind man continued with amusement, "I always forget that others might need light when I do not. The only good thing about these," he added, waving the torch, "is that they warm me up when it's cold."

With that, the torch took light and flared up.

"Is that better?" he asked.

Aghiles and Blandula had no time to reply before four men jumped them. In an instant, one of them had taken hold of

121

Blandula's arm and slapped a hand over her mouth. The three others slammed Aghiles against the wall and held him there. Normally, the Numidian giant would have overcome them with no problem, but their assailants had the advantage of surprise. Aghiles only had time to strike one in the head before he found himself pushed violently against the wall. He struggled with all his might and struck out at one of his attackers, but still couldn't manage to get free of their hold.

"Aaaargh!" he screamed in fury.

Blandula's eyes rolled in terror. With that, the icy tone of the caretaker broke in, revealing a totally different personality.

"Who are you?! What are you really looking for?"

"For Cornelius!" wailed Aghiles.

"Do you think just a name is enough for me to trust you? There's many a Cornelius in Rome…" The old man's face had suddenly turned hard as stone.

Aghiles looked about him as best as he could in his hapless position. He could see Blandula's look of terror. He stifled a groan of fury. Why hadn't he been more suspicious? He had thought they were safe from a blind man. He had to admit, the trick had worked: they had walked straight into the jaws of the lion.

"Who are you?" the blind man repeated. "Who sent you?"

"No one. We've come to pay our respects to Master Cornelius."

"Respects!" sneered the caretaker. "Now confess you're in the pay of the emperor and his henchmen!"

"No! It's the truth!"

"Ha, the truth! Okay, I'll wait."

"Wait for what?!" groaned the Numidian.

"The password. If you're really among our friends, you should know it."

Aghiles finally got it: a password. He had thought of everything, but not that.

"I'm waiting!"

Blandula looked from Aghiles to the blind man with a haunted look. She was frightened, and her eyes filled with tears. The man with his hand over her mouth had been watching in silence all this time. But now he broke silence. "Augustus!" he shouted.

The caretaker turned to the sound of his voice.

"Listen to the girl. I wonder if maybe…"

The old man hesitated, and then raised his hand in a signal to his accomplice to let go of her mouth. Blandula gulped, gasping for air.

"Who are you?" the caretaker sharply questioned her.

"I told you. My name is Blandula, and I came here to pay my respects to my master, Cornelius. He was taken away a few days ago, and I know that he was put to death, in the Colosseum. I wasn't there at the games, but I was told about it. Ever since then, I've been searching for where they took him. I want to be sure he had a decent burial."

Augustus twisted his mouth. "And the password?"

"What password?!" roared Aghiles. "We didn't know we needed a password. We're not Christians."

"In that case, how did you know to come here? There are cemeteries all over the city, and many Christian catacombs in several places. So why come here?"

"I was told I'd find him here," said Blandula.

"Who told you?"

Blandula hesitated and cast an eye toward Aghiles, who frowned. One of the men holding him saw his look and twisted his arm behind his back. Aghiles groaned.

"One of your people," Blandula blurted out. "Aghiles here and his friends saved his life."

Augustus gave a doubtful smile. "You're a very clever little liar. I don't buy your fine stories."

"I swear, it's true. He was left behind in the Colosseum."

One of the men raised an eyebrow and asked. "In the Colosseum, did you say?"

"Blandula!" Aghiles thundered, trying to keep her quiet.

But she had already said too much. And their lives now hung on what she would say next. "The guards left him there to die."

"And do you know what his name might be?"

"Paulus," replied Blandula. "His name is Paulus."

The man who had spoken stared at her in disbelief. "Paulus is alive?!"

Without even realizing, he had loosened his grip on Aghiles. That was all Aghiles needed. Like lightning, he freed his arm and smashed his fist into the man's face. He dislocated the jaw of the second with a jab of his elbow and overpowered the third before he had time to react. But the one holding Blandula gripped her even more tightly.

"Let her go," growled Aghiles.

The man shook his head.

"Let her go!" the Numidian menaced.

"Enough! Stop!" The blind man's thunderous shout echoed through the little crypt. "If Paulus is alive, these people are our friends."

XXIX

ANGER

"So?" Fulgur's tone was sharp.

"They're at the house of someone called Cornelius, an old magistrate."

"Hmm! Any links with the emperor's police?"

The boy informant shook his head. "No, but..."

"But what?"

"Old Cornelius doesn't live there anymore."

"What are you talking about?"

"He was arrested a few days ago."

When Fulgur remained silent, he went on.

"He was a Christian. He was killed in the Colosseum."

"So what are they doing there then?"

The boy didn't dare answer.

"What are they doing there?!"

The boy bowed his head. "We don't know," he whimpered.

Fulgur's hand came down on his ear with a resounding slap. The blow stung him before he had time to duck. The boy tottered to the side, off balance. Fulgur grabbed him by the hair and forced him to kneel down before him. The boy put his hand to his stinging ear and shrank back in terror.

"You dare come to report that you don't know?"

The boy said nothing. What good would it do to say anything more? He gritted his teeth and awaited the next blow.

But the blow didn't come. Fulgur was thinking.

"Find out what's going on in that house," he said at last. "If they've got something to hide, I need to know. You got that?"

The boy nodded and ran off before Fulgur could strike him again.

XXX

LAST RESPECTS

"Paulus is one of us," explained Augustus, suddenly more talkative. "He was ill when they arrested him. He didn't appear in the circus arena, and unfortunately none of his cellmates survived to tell us what happened to him. We had lost all hope of him, but if you tell us he's alive, that's wonderful news. Very great news. Our little community needs him. Where is he?"

"In my house," said Blandula. "At least, I mean, in my master's old house."

"We'll arrange to come get him." The old man paused before continuing, "Thank you for having saved his life. And," he added to Aghiles, "please forgive this heavy-handed welcome."

"He packs a good punch himself!" added one of the men.

Aghiles smiled despite himself: it's true, he hadn't pulled his punches.

"We're wary of strangers. Despite people's fear of even the word *Christian*, we get many curiosity-seekers. It's easy to get rid of them quickly. But some, like you, are more insistent. If they know the password, we know we can trust them. If not, we have to suspect they've come to spy on us. Some people are ready to do anything to denounce Christians. Informants hope it will win them favor and help them reach high positions of state."

Augustus turned his head in disgust. "They stop at nothing. Some even come with children to convince us of their good faith. So our little welcoming committee is here to make sure they never come back."

Blandula went white as a sheet. "You kill them?" she asked.

"The Lord tells us: 'You shall not kill.' No, we don't harm them. We simply scare them off. They're never suspicious of me," Augustus added with a smile. "It's child's play taking them by surprise."

Aghiles winced. What a fool he'd been to let himself be taken in like a child.

"And Cornelius?" Blandula timidly asked. "Is he really here?"

"Yes, he's in the dormitory."

The girl stiffened and took a step back.

"In…in the dormitory?" she stammered. "But you told me he was dead."

The old man smiled gently and shook his head. "Your master is indeed dead, my girl. And he's buried in the dormitory along with his own. We call our cemetery a dormitory because we are only destined to repose there for a short while."

"And then you move your dead?"

"No, no! But we Christians believe in the resurrection."

Since neither Blandula nor Aghiles seemed to understand, he went on. "One day, we will all live again. Death will be vanquished. It will then be nothing more than a kind of long rest in the dormitory."

Blandula frowned. She didn't understand it all, but out of respect for her master, she remained silent.

"Follow me."

The blind man raised the torch he had been holding all this time and lit up the ceiling. Aghiles' and Blandula's eyes opened wide in wonderment.

Until that moment, they hadn't noticed what was all around them. The underground gallery they were in, carved out of the white, chalky stone, was astonishing. It glinted in the light. Colorful frescoes decorated the walls. They could see a shepherd with his sheep, guests seated at a long table, fish, women's faces…

"Follow me," the old caretaker repeated.

He handed the torch to Aghiles standing next to him and disappeared into a dark, narrow passageway. Everywhere, on all sides, the flame of the torch revealed long niches carved into the stone and closed up with bricks or big stone plaques. Some of them were engraved with symbols.

"Christians ask to be buried here," the caretaker explained. "Those fortunate enough to have a larger tomb are few and far between. We prefer to repose next to one another, like brothers and sisters of the same family. We are all children of God through our baptism."

Blandula and Aghiles listened without comment. This all seemed very mysterious to them.

They finally emerged into another slightly larger room with many corridors leading off it. They could see a flickering light at the end of one of them.

The caretaker stopped and turned to Blandula. "Your master is in this gallery," he told her. "I don't know if his name has been engraved on the stone. At the end, you'll find a man who closes up the most recent tombs. You can ask him."

The girl hesitated and moved a step closer to Aghiles. Without a word, he grabbed her hand and led her down the narrow corridor.

"It's good that you came," the caretaker said to them.

After the welcome they had received, this remark seemed odd. But Blandula immediately understood what the old man meant. It was good for her to see that her master had been properly buried in a peaceful place. When she reached the spot, there was such a serene atmosphere. She now knew that her master was at peace.

XXXI

THREATS

The pounding echoed through the whole villa. Paulus, Maximus, and Titus jumped. They looked at one another without a word. A heavy silence fell on the room. Then the pounding started again. The walls seemed to shake.

"Open up!" The shout came from the street.

Maximus' gaze swept the room, summing up the situation. "Soldiers," he murmured. They had to be quick.

A look of terror crossed Titus' face. Paulus, however, remained strangely calm.

"We must hide," whispered Maximus.

He looked questioningly at Paulus. "Can you walk?"

Maximus automatically included him in their escape plans. The idea of taking advantage of the situation to abandon him to his fate, as he had thought of doing the night before, no longer even crossed his mind.

Paulus smiled weakly. "I'll only slow you down," he said. "You go! Leave me here. It's nothing more than what's been in store for me all along."

When Maximus didn't move but instead went on looking for a solution, Paulus insisted. "Go! Look after Blandula. She took a great risk for me. Get her to safety."

This time, Maximus nodded. He looked Paulus straight in the eye. His cool-headedness was impressive. "Good luck," he said. Then, dragging Titus behind him, he left the bedroom.

The banging on the door grew louder.

"He could talk and betray us," Titus worried. "We…"

"Open up!" a voice again thundered from outside.

"To the roof!" shouted Maximus.

Like most Roman villas, the house was built around a central atrium, the patio with the fountain where they had washed. The two boys ran there. Maximus immediately spotted the olive tree. It was planted a couple of feet away from the wall, but it was close enough to get onto the roof. He signaled to Titus, climbed the tree, and jumped. He made it.

But the tip of his thick sandal caught the edge of the roof. He tripped and then slipped backward toward the edge. His legs dangled in midair, his one hand clutching the roof ledge.

Maximus swung dangerously. He braced his body. He focused his mind. He grabbed the rooftop with the fingertips of his other hand. Then, with one mighty effort, he hoisted himself up to his elbows, and then swung himself up onto the roof terrace. Just as he was regaining his balance, he was jolted by a battering ram at the street door. The cracking wood could be heard through the whole house. Maximus leaned down over the edge and stretched his hand down to Titus, still climbing up the olive tree. He was just out of reach of his fingertips. But Titus suddenly leapt up. Maximus caught his arm and pulled him to safety.

After all their exhausting and dangerous gymnastics, they were joined by pesky little Dux, who scampered up to them in just a few leaps and bounds.

Downstairs the wooden door gave way. Titus and Maximus laid as flat on the rooftop as they could and held their breath, hoping the olive tree would shield them from being seen.

They could hear men running through the house. They heard the clinking of arms, footsteps clattering on the flagstones. Orders were shouted out all over. Objects smashed to the ground. Maximus struggled to hear what was happening. He heard yelling, curses. Several times men crisscrossed the patio, clawing through the potted plants. One man even climbed the first few branches of the olive tree to make sure no one was hiding there, and then gave up. The search seemed to go on forever. They can't have found Paulus, thought Maximus, unless he had already denounced them and the soldiers were now searching for them!

At last, all of the guards gathered in the patio.

"Nothing!"

"No one!"

"They've fled."

"But an empty bed is still warm!"

Maximus stared wide-eyed and turned to Titus, who couldn't understand any more than he did.

When silence once again settled on the house, Paulus came out of his hiding place with a groan. It was a miracle: the soldiers hadn't found him.

When it had become obvious that the emperor's emissaries wouldn't content themselves with remaining in the street, he had grabbed the book of the Gospels and slipped to the foot of the bed with a wince of pain. Then, he had slowly inched under the bed and curled up in a ball with the book pressed to his heart. He closed his eyes and prayed the soldiers wouldn't find him.

They had entered the room several times. They had searched everywhere. One of them had even bent down to look under the bed. And each time, they had left empty-handed!

XXXII

PANIC

Victor was in a panic. When he saw the soldiers arrive and go into Master Cornelius' villa, he feared the worst. But then they came out. Alone. Victor heard them saying the house was empty. What a disaster! Fulgur would never forgive him for losing the trail of the boys. To say nothing of the Numidian who had managed to slip away earlier. For a long time, a troop at the top of the road had barred Victor's passage. When at last it had been safe for him to approach, the slave and his girl companion had disappeared.

Victor wrung his hands and looked about in despair. Why did this always happen to him? He was cursed. In the end, that *bulla* had caused him nothing but trouble. He grabbed it, hidden under his tunic. He pulled on its chain but hesitated before ripping it off. On reflection, that might just make things worse.

Victor thought quickly. He would have a little time before the relief guard arrived. If he stayed there, he would have to admit his failure, and go tell Fulgur. His rage would be terrible. Victor trembled at the very thought of it. He had heard about his gang leader's temper. The boys spoke about it under their breath, their eyes filled with fear, their voices quivering. He had apparently killed a man. Maybe two, even. Victor wasn't sure.

But whatever the case, he didn't want to be the next one on the list. What if he were just to disappear?

One thing was certain: Fulgur would be furious. But Victor wouldn't be there to see it. Of course, that would mean returning to a life of misery, like before, but at least he would still be alive. And then—who knows?—maybe with a bit of luck he would find the boys again. Then everything would go back to normal. He would go back to Fulgur. He would explain how he had followed the targets and had no time to let him know. Fulgur would congratulate him. Maybe even forgive him. It would be his moment of glory. The start of a new life.

Victor hesitated not a moment longer. He gave one last look at the house behind him and ran away.

XXXIII

EMERGENCY

Aghiles looked around. He thought he had heard someone calling him. He squeezed Blandula's hand and carried on through the crowd. If only there weren't so many people, they would get there quicker. Aghiles rushed. He was in a hurry to find his friends and announce the good news: they had found a solution for Paulus. A simple solution that would surely please everyone. Paulus above all, but Maximus as well.

"Aghiles!"

This time, Aghiles stopped. He was sure someone was calling his name. He searched the crowd around him and gave a little start when someone laid a hand on his arm. He turned and recognized his friend's blond mop. "Maximus? But..."

"I was watching out for you," Maximus whispered. "Titus is on the other side of the road." Maximus looked around, on the alert. He spoke quickly. "The soldiers came."

Blandula went pale.

"You can't go back home. Someone must have betrayed you."

"And Paulus?" asked Aghiles.

"He told us to go hide because he was too weak to keep up with us. He stayed in the bedroom, but the soldiers didn't find him."

"No! Really?"

Maximus nodded his head.

"And you?" Blandula asked.

"Us?"

"Yes, did you find him?"

Maximus frowned. "We didn't look. We got away over the rooftops. At all costs, we had to warn you not to go back."

"Is the house being watched?" Aghiles asked.

"I don't know. But there were so many of them, it's possible."

"We must go see," Blandula said suddenly.

Aghiles and Maximus stared at her in amazement.

"Paulus couldn't have disappeared just like that. Nor made an escape," she pleaded. "You said yourself, he's too weak. He must still be in the house. We have to help him."

Maximus cleared his throat. Since the soldiers had left, he had been thinking. This mysterious disappearance of Paulus suited him perfectly. It meant he wouldn't have to make a decision about what to do with him. Yet Maximus had felt his determination dissolving. Paulus seemed to him an honest, upright man. And, then, he hadn't discovered anything about him that deserved the pain of death. His only crime had been his refusal to believe in the Roman gods. He was guilty of nothing more than rejecting the religion of the Roman people. But, after all, Maximus didn't fully accept it either. Since he didn't practice it, was he a criminal too?

"I'm sure he's still inside," Blandula insisted. "We have to go look for him and get him out of there so he can join his friends."

"His friends?" asked Maximus.

Aghiles nodded. "It's a long story, and this isn't the place to discuss it. How can we get back into the house?"

Maximus frowned. It was clear he was never going to convince his friends to forget about Paulus. "They broke down the front door," he said. "That's how the soldiers got in. There's still the little lane in the back, or the rooftops. But it's too risky to go back into the villa. With the front door open, anyone may have gotten in. We could be taken at any moment."

They walked as they spoke, keeping a close eye on everything around them. As they approached the house of Master Cornelius, Blandula bowed her head and pulled her veil down over her head, hoping to avoid the eye of anyone who might recognize her. She gave a little cry on seeing the broken door. When the soldiers smashed in the wood, the door had come off its hinges. It was a chilling sight.

Gritting his teeth, Maximus walked on as though nothing were wrong. After a few steps, he explained to his friends what he was thinking. "As long as it's still daylight, no one will dare go in," he observed. "They're afraid. They'll be frightened of being arrested if they try anything. But once night falls, thieves and curiosity-seekers won't hesitate."

He paused and turned to Blandula with a deeply apologetic look. "They'll ransack everything. By tomorrow, I'm afraid there won't remain much of your master's villa."

Blandula was dismayed: it was as though Master Cornelius were dying all over again. "That means we don't have much time if we want to get back in and find Paulus," she cried. "After that, it will be too late."

Aghiles spotted Titus and signaled to him to join them. Soon, their number was complete.

Realizing that Blandula and Aghiles would never leave Paulus in the villa, Maximus resigned himself to helping them. "To get back into the villa, we have to be quick," he said. "We'll go back in over the rooftops the same way Titus and I got out. Blandula will gather up whatever she wants to save, while we search for Paulus—in the hope he's still to be found. Then we get out and take him somewhere safe."

"We found Paulus' friends," whispered Blandula. "If we take him to them, they'll know what to do."

Now that seemed like a good idea. If others took the invalid off his hands, Maximus would no longer be in danger. "Where is it?" he asked.

"In the catacombs."

Maximus winced. "That's far. Paulus will never be able to make it there on foot, and…"

"…and if Aghiles carried him, we'd be spotted right away," Titus finished his sentence.

As he said this, there was suddenly agitation in the crowd around them.

"Make way! Out of the way!" The command made them jump. Maximus, Titus, Aghiles, and Blandula automatically stepped to one side, against the wall of a building.

A man hurried past them, moving the people before him out of the way. "Make way!" he yelled.

Two men were following a few yards behind him, and another two behind them.

They were carrying a long, curtained bed, called a litter, on which sat a woman of the Roman nobility, half-hidden from the crowd behind blue curtains.

"But of course," exclaimed Titus, "a litter! I'll take care of finding one for us. Leave it to me!"

XXXIV

THE WORKSHOP

"Is anyone there?" called Titus.

The shop was piled up with planks of wood, blocks of stone, bolts of fabric, huge pots, heavy pieces of metal, and, above all, dust.

"Apicius?" Titus' voice was lost in the noise coming from the back room. The air echoed with hammering on metal.

"Apicius?!"

Titus stepped carefully forward. In this workshop of his father's friend, a person never knew what he might step on. It was like a true curiosity shop.

"Api…"

"Titus!"

The boy gave a start. Apicius had emerged from behind a pile of stage props. On seeing him, Titus gave a smile. This crafts-man was a real curiosity in and of himself. He was very tall, with straggly, slightly dirty hair, his face forever covered in fine white dust. He wore a short, patched tunic. He looked like one of those poor beggars selling wilted flowers in the markets. And yet, Apicius wasn't poor. He was in fact rather rich—very rich. But his appearance was the least of his concerns, and when he was at work in his shop, he especially didn't give a hoot what he looked like.

"Titus! What brings you here?"

Apicius had worked for years with Titus' father. They regularly worked together on shows for the wealthy notables of the city and often helped each other out when they needed some object or some animal or other. Titus was used to visiting Apicius on errands for his father. So there was nothing surprising in his visit today.

"We need a litter."

Titus didn't go into any details. The less Apicius knew, the less chance his father had of finding out he had visited his colleague in his name.

"A litter?" The man raised a curious eyebrow, scratched his head—ruffling his wild hair even more—and cast an eye on the bric-a-brac around him.

Apicius was the official supplier of stage props for all the city's theaters. Costumes, plants, terra cotta statues of the gods, and painted billboards, as well as vehicles of all sorts—he could put his hands on anything at a moment's notice. A few others had tried to compete in the same market with him, but without success. Apicius was a real workhorse who spent almost all his time in the workshop cobbling together curious machines, making copies of sculptures, building huge models of entire cities in wood, or forging fake weapons in metal. No one could match his skill, his business sense, his network of suppliers, or his team of workmen in every field imaginable.

"I've already rented most of them out," he said, thinking out loud. "I think…maybe…unless…What about Cleopatra's litter?"

"Perfect! That's perfect!"

"Cleopatra's? Are you sure?"

"Absolutely! It's only to help us out for a few hours. And could you get me two mules to carry it too? We'll bring it all back tomorrow."

Apicius gave him a broad smile. "You'd be better off asking your father for two slaves to carry it. My mules are particularly stubborn."

Titus wrinkled his nose. "No, it has to be animals. But my father's are all a little too…exotic!"

Apicius nodded. No point asking any more questions. He knew, like Titus' father, that one doesn't argue with a client's requirements. Over time, he had learned to be surprised at nothing and simply to meet all orders, even the craziest.

"Fine! Go around back. My man will sort you out. And hey! Tell your father I need a camel for next week!"

Titus nodded and said, "Consider it done!"

He thanked Apicius, who had already gotten back to work, and walked around the block. The little courtyard at the back of Apicius' studio was even more piled up with stuff than the shop where the celebrated craftsman received his customers. Titus sat down on a wooden throne with a red baldachin and waited.

His amused gaze wandered idly from object to object: all fakes, copies, cobbled-together imitations. Close up, you could see the slapdash repairs, the wobbly hinges, the defects, and the clumsy drawings. For example, the throne he was sitting on was full of splinters and cracks. But, from a distance, it created a perfect illusion. Apicius hadn't built his reputation on the finish of his stage props, but on their appearance of authenticity and, above all, on his ability to fill any order on short notice.

Suddenly, a furious braying made Titus start.

"Go on! Giddyap!" said a man guiding a mule through piles of props, dragging behind it a litter attached to another mule. The curious transport squeaked and squealed, got stuck, and then twisted and turned. At last, the pile of stuff gave way and the litter lurched forward, smacking the rump of the mule in front. It reared up in surprise.

"Whoa! Easy does it!" his handler soothed him.

Once the litter was finally clear and the animals calmed down, the man turned with a smile to Titus. "Cleopatra's litter! This for you?"

Titus took a good look, gulped, and then nodded his head, speechless.

XXXV

A MIRACULOUS SURVIVOR

Maximus had no trouble finding the place where he and Titus had come down from the roof earlier that day. It was a narrow alley between two villas. It was dark and stank to high heaven. Every cat and dog in the neighborhood must have been using it to do their business! At least that had one advantage: it was completely deserted.

Maximus went into the tiny alley first, followed by Blandula and Aghiles, who checked that they hadn't been followed. At the end of the alley, the slave bent down against the wall, cradled his hands together, and signaled to Maximus to climb up. Maximus was used to this: he put one foot in Aghiles' hands and grabbed his shoulders. When the giant stood and raised his cupped hands, Maximus was almost at roof-level. He grabbed the edge and, with one good last boost from Aghiles, hoisted himself up and over. Aghiles then turned to Blandula. The girl smiled at him and placed her foot in his hands. When the slave lifted her up, he was surprised: she was as light as a feather. Up on the roof, Maximus grasped Blandula's hand to help her up.

"What about Aghiles?" she asked as she set foot on the roof terrace.

Maximus smiled. "Don't worry about him, he always manages!"

Blandula turned and watched as the strapping young man climbed up. Bracing one hand on each wall, and then both his feet, crab-like, he nimbly made his way up. Within seconds, he had joined them on the roof.

"Quick!" said Maximus. "There's no time to lose!"

Bent over in order not to be seen from the street, the three crept rapidly forward to the house of Master Cornelius. Blandula couldn't hide her surprise on seeing the patio from above. She'd never noticed the carefully clipped bushes and the neat straight lines of gravel. Unbeknownst to her, it all formed a kind of picture designed to be seen from the heavens. Blandula smiled at the thought that her master was looking down on her from the place he had hoped to go.

Maximus carefully scoured the courtyard below, on the alert for the slightest suspicious movement, the slightest little noise. After a long pause, he at last turned around to Aghiles and Blandula and whispered, "I think we can go now, but be quiet! No one in the street must suspect there's anyone in the house. Blandula, you gather up what you need… but not too much. While you do that, we'll try to find Paulus."

Blandula's face clouded over. "And what if we don't find him?"

"That's more than likely," said Maximus gently, trying to prepare her for the worst.

Blandula bowed her head. "All right, let's go," she whispered.

Aghiles slipped silently down to the ground, squatted there for a moment listening, and then rose and signaled to Maximus to help Blandula down. She landed in the arms of Aghiles, who set her down. Maximus followed behind her. Without a word, the three headed straight for Blandula's bedroom.

The room was empty. Paulus wasn't in the bed. The sheets had been torn aside and thrown on the floor. It was the same with Blandula's few belongings. The soldiers had ransacked everything along their way. Blandula stifled a gasp as she spotted Paulus lying on the floor next to the bed. He hadn't had the strength to raise himself back onto it.

"Paulus!" She rushed to him, with Maximus and Aghiles right behind her.

Indeed, it was Paulus. As pale as death but smiling. "You came back," he murmured. "My prayers were heard."

"But the soldiers…," Maximus wondered. "They searched everywhere."

Paulus nodded, beaming despite his extreme fatigue. "I know. But somehow they didn't see me."

Maximus was flabbergasted. But this wasn't the moment for explanations. "Right!" he said. "We must hurry. It will soon be nightfall, and we have to be there when Titus arrives with the litter. Aghiles, can you carry Paulus?"

"To the patio, yes. But I'll need help hoisting him onto the roof."

"Blandula, we'll need sheets," Maximus shouted. "Lots of sheets!"

She nodded and immediately disappeared to the other end of the house. In each room she passed, she grabbed the sheets and anything that could help. Just when she was about to return to the boys, she stopped. She had just remembered Master Cornelius' togas, those long robes several yards in length. So she headed for her master's bedroom.

Before going in, she tapped lightly on the door—it was an instinct, an old habit…but perhaps it was also in the secret hope that this had all been a bad dream and the raspy voice of Master Cornelius would ask her to come in. After a few seconds, she at last decided to open the door.

Even though the soldiers had knocked everything over, nothing had changed in the room. Blandula shook herself, not wanting to give in to emotion. She went to the chest that sat by the wall. That was where Cornelius had kept his personal belongings. Without hesitation, she grabbed four magnificent, immaculately white togas, rolled them up under her arm, and left.

When she returned to her bedroom, Paulus was no longer there. She found him on the patio with Aghiles and Maximus. The boys grabbed the togas and hurried to wrap Paulus up in them, leaving a large border free on both sides. They worked quickly and silently. Aghiles never stopped shooting worried looks toward the part of the courtyard closest to the front door. He feared they would be taken by surprise.

When everything was ready, they climbed into the olive tree, each dragging one end of the toga behind them. They jumped onto the roof and gently pulled their package up. Paulus was soon suspended in mid-air in the improvised hammock. Gradually, as gently as they could, they lifted him up. After several long and exhausting minutes, Aghiles managed to hoist their load up onto the roof. Blandula and Maximus both joined them. Aghiles gave each of them his arm to help them jump across.

When all four of them were at last back on the terrace, they breathed a sigh of relief. Aghiles was about to put Paulus on his back and head back over the roof to the meeting point with Titus when he realized Blandula had come back out empty-handed.

"But your things? Where are your belongings?"

The girl hadn't had the time to gather up anything.

"I'll go back down, if you like?"

Blandula shook her head. "No," she said, "it's too dangerous. It's not important. And, in any case, I have a new life before me."

She shivered as she spoke those words: a new life indeed, full of the unknown and of danger. She hadn't the slightest idea where she would go.

"Don't worry," Maximus told her. "We won't let you down."

"Let's get going!" said Blandula energetically, trying to chase away her gloomy thoughts. "Titus will be waiting for us!"

XXXVI

BATTLE STATIONS!

The soldiers moved on the double. They grabbed their weapons, checked their shields, belted up their tunics and sandals, and adjusted their helmets. The atmosphere in the barracks was electric. You could feel the hum of excitement. So it wasn't a rumor after all. It was really happening. The attack was on for that night.

In the corner of the large room, one soldier was preparing more slowly than the others. He was worried. He hadn't had time to warn Flavia. The order had taken him by surprise. There had been no reason to suppose the attack would be this evening. It was in the air; rumors had swelled through the ranks, but nothing precise.

Flavia's brother smiled bitterly. He had to admit the strategy was clever. By keeping the soldiers in the dark, the officers had avoided any leaks. And, therefore, any failure. They wanted this night raid to be a complete success. And they had done everything to make sure it would be.

Everything had been prepared down to the last detail and kept perfectly secret. The attack would take place simultaneously in all the Christian cemeteries. Every garrison of soldiers and watchmen had been mobilized, except for two needed to patrol the streets as usual. The element of surprise would be total. No one would escape.

The next games were to be held in a few weeks. One thing was sure: there would be plenty of fresh Christians for the lions. The emperor would be pleased.

XXXVII

COMPLETE DISCRETION

Maximus was getting impatient. Titus had still not arrived. Crouching in the shadows of the narrow alleyway, they were all on the verge of suffocating...even though they were all holding an edge of their tunic over their noses. By the end of the day, the stench was absolutely horrible.

"What the heck is he doing?" Maximus grumbled with exasperation. He had hoped they could just melt into the crowd, but little by little the street was emptying. If Titus didn't hurry up, the streets would be deserted.

At last, they could make out the sound of hooves clip-clopping in the distance. Maximus strained his ears. He signaled to the others to be at the ready. But they needed to be careful. Earlier they had nearly jumped out of their hiding place, but the litter going by didn't slow down at the end of the alley—as Titus had said it would. Sure enough, it wasn't Titus.

Aghiles, still holding Paulus in his arms, gave a sigh of relief. He lifted his charge onto his shoulder, while Blandula covered him up with a toga, making Paulus look like any other ordinary sack of goods.

The clip-clopping came closer. It seemed to be slowing down. Maximus looked to Aghiles with a smile. Titus had done it! He knew they could count on him!

When the first mule's head finally appeared at the end of the alley, Maximus could hear his friend's voice calling the animal to halt.

"Whoa!"

Maximus cast a last look behind him at Aghiles and Blandula and signaled to them to be quick. They would have only a few seconds to put Paulus into the litter. They had agreed that the litter would just slow down without coming to a full stop. They didn't want any passersby to think someone had gotten in along the way.

When the top of the litter, flanked by roaring lions, came into view, Maximus gave a start and hesitated for a moment. But Titus rushed to his side.

"Quick! Hurry up!" he said.

Aghiles took a couple of steps forward and laid his charge in the litter behind its curtains. In the blink of an eye, Blandula had joined Paulus in this strange conveyance. Maximus had thought it better that way, so as not to run the risk of anyone recognizing her.

The whole operation was completed in seconds. The mules had hardly even had time to slow down; no one had noticed their passage. But several people did give an amused look at this funny litter.

"It's Cleopatra's litter," explained Titus, out of breath.

Aghiles followed behind them. The giant Numidian kept a watchful eye on this strange procession, bemused but with a straight face.

"You must be joking!" Maximus groaned through his teeth.

"What? You asked for a litter, and I found you one! You think it's easy to find a litter at a moment's notice? And free of charge, may I remind you!"

"Yeah, but talk about discretion…are you kidding?!"

Maximus examined the thing and rolled his eyes. True, Titus was right: it *was* a litter—but oh, what a litter! Its two uprights were surmounted by gilt lions with gaping jaws. Its tentlike canopy, topped by a golden pyramid on four sculpted feet, sheltered the litter from the weather. The curtains, supposedly there to protect the occupant from public view, were sheer white, almost transparent. One would think Cleopatra liked being carried around the streets as though she were on stage! The forms of Paulus and Blandula were clearly visible. And that of Dux as well, for the little monkey hadn't waited for his master's permission to slip inside with them. In the end, maybe it wasn't such a bad thing that Titus had taken so long. The falling darkness might help mask the journey of this outrageous contraption.

"Which way are we going?" Titus asked.

"The Appian Way. To the south. To the cemeteries..."

XXXVIII

IMPATIENCE

Fulgur was pacing up and down. He was waiting. And he *hated* waiting.

"What are those boys doing?!" he yelled.

Victor should have already been there to report. But he still hadn't shown up. And the boy who was supposed to take over Victor's watch should have returned to say that Victor was missing—if he was missing. Fulgur didn't know where the boys were or what they were up to. Or rather, yes, he could imagine. They must be hiding. The little scoundrels had hidden somewhere instead of coming to bring him the news. So it must be bad news. A man didn't need to be born from Jupiter's thigh to figure that out.

Fulgur couldn't just stand there doing nothing, biting his nails. He grabbed his long dagger and stuck it in his belt. Then he covered his head with a fold of his tunic and left. As he passed the guard posted at the Ludus Magnus, the gladiators' big barracks, Fulgur gave him a silent, slight nod of the head. The guard stood aside to let him pass.

The two of them had known each other a long time. They had come to a sort of arrangement that suited them both. In exchange for a nice sum of money each week, a ration of sausages, and, above all, those little good-luck charms he was so fond of, the guard closed his eyes and kept his mouth shut about the gang. Fulgur made use of the little room that had been his when he had been a gladiator, and his boys were able to enter through the Ludus Magnus when entry through the Colosseum wasn't possible.

Once out on the street, Fulgur immediately scurried toward the villa of Master Cornelius. "If you want something done, better do it yourself," he muttered under his breath.

He had decided to take things into his own hands. And those useless boys of his will be sorry when he gets his hands on them!

XXXIX

CLEOPATRA'S LITTER

Kneeling in the litter, Blandula settled Paulus as comfortably as possible. Each bump in the road made him wince in pain. Fortunately, their litter enclosure was fitted with several red and gold cushions. Blandula supported his back with them. Then she covered him with lengths of colorful fabric. She tried to mask his terrible thinness. If anyone stopped them, Paulus would have to pass for a wealthy notable on his way home.

"Thank you, Blandula," he whispered.

Without a word, she simply gave him a smile. She looked after him gently, chasing Dux away from time to time with the back of her hand when he bothered Paulus. The little monkey was entranced by the pompoms on the cushions and kept trying to play with them.

"Are you frightened?" he asked.

Blandula shook her head. "I'd rather not think about it."

"The Lord will help us, you'll see."

Blandula gave him a doubtful look. She didn't want to hurt Paulus' feelings, but she doubted that his god could do much in this situation. He hadn't saved her master's life. They'd better just count on themselves.

Outside the curtains, Maximus, Titus, and Aghiles walked at the mules' pace, trying to look as natural as possible. But they were extremely tense; Maximus above all. When he saw the

159

astonished looks of the passersby at the sight of their contraption, he realized just how mad this plan was. All he had wanted was to avoid causing his father any problems, and now here he was walking straight into the jaws of the lion. He cursed himself for letting his friends persuade him, for not taking a firmer stand right from the start.

Everything would have been so much simpler if they had just left Paulus in his cell…when the prisoner still meant nothing to him. Now, it was too late. He knew too much about this Christian to turn his back on him. It was out of the question to abandon him and his friends at this point. He wasn't a coward. It was a matter of his honor to see this thing through—in the hope it would all end well.

Titus too was extremely nervous, but for different reasons. The team of mules he had borrowed were hopeless. They refused to obey. They kept stopping for no reason, turning in the wrong direction. Between them, the litter sometimes tilted dangerously to one side and kept making grinding noises. Titus was pulling his hair out and calling on every god he could name.

Suddenly, a passerby more curious than the rest approached them and asked, "Isn't that Cleopatra's litter?"

Titus nodded with a groan.

"Are you actors, then?"

"Mmm," Titus mumbled, hoping to shake off this nosy man.

"You must be on your way to the celebrations at Senator Agrippa's," the man continued.

Titus was about to reply when he thought better of it. It was too risky. He let the man prattle on.

"You know, Agrippa—the senator. He's giving a party tonight, and he's promised us a surprise." When Titus remained silent, the man gave him a knowing little smile. "Ahh! I get it! You're not saying anything because I've guessed correctly, haven't I!" he said, pleased with himself.

Maximus cleared his throat. "Excuse us," he said.

"I'm right, aren't I?" the man insisted.

"Please don't put us in a difficult situation," Maximus continued. "We're sworn to secrecy."

"Well, now that I know what he's up to, I'll know how to surprise him," the man snickered. "I'll outdo that crafty old Agrippa! He's always bragging about how he knows best how to surprise his guests. Well, not this time!" Without another word, he moved on, delighted.

"Well, there goes someone who'll get more than one surprise this evening!" laughed Titus.

"That's for sure! But in the meantime, he's given us a perfect alibi. From now on, if anyone asks, all we have to say is that we're on our way to Senator Agrippa's party."

"Where does he live?" asked Titus.

Maximus shrugged his shoulders. "No idea. I don't even know who he is. But it's enough to know about his party to explain our presence—especially with this rig, out in the street at this hour."

Pleased with himself, Maximus slowed his pace to whisper this new information to Blandula and Paulus, and then to Aghiles.

As he let the curtain fall again over the litter, Paulus smiled as he looked at Blandula. "And so now we've become actors!" he said with a laugh. "The Lord has a good sense of humor!"

Blandula looked at him, her head to one side. "You think it's your god who arranged this?"

"Who else?" Paulus spoke with such confidence, the girl was taken aback. "I believe that God is present in each moment of my life."

161

"You're not resentful?" Blandula couldn't help but remark. "He hasn't exactly been much help to you lately."

"He sent you to me."

"And what about all those who died, what about them? Was your god with them? And my master, Cornelius?" Blandula's tone was sharp, almost furious.

Paulus gravely shook his head. "As strange as it may seem to you, yes, I believe the Lord was with them. He was by their side, supporting them in their fear and suffering. Think of how they smiled in death."

Blandula shook her head and closed her eyes. "I can't go to the circus games," she said. "It's too cruel. I never saw anyone smile at the hour of their death."

Paulus remained silent for a long moment. Then, with a distant look, he went on, "We're never alone, Blandula. That I can promise you."

At that moment, the bizarre cavalcade began to turn into a side street when Titus pulled on the reins to stop the mule in front. Roman soldiers were patrolling just ahead. They would have to go another way.

"Whoa! Whoa!" Titus ordered the animal.

For once, the mule in front obeyed. But the pesky one behind kept going, ignoring Maximus' shouts. It rammed the whole litter into the lead mule's rump with such a jolt, it brayed in fright, attracting everyone's attention. With that, the soldier closing the ranks of the Roman patrol stopped short and turned around—just in time to spot Titus and the mule he was desperately tugging at disappearing around the corner.

"Hey! You there!" he shouted.

XL

DESERTED!

Not a soul! It was just as Fulgur expected. None of his men were on watch at the house of Cornelius. And, what's worse, the villa's front door had been broken down. Fulgur didn't know what had happened, but it didn't look good. That door could only be the work of soldiers. And if they had arrested the three boys, that was very bad. He knew better than anyone: it was amazing how fear could loosen tongues. That was the tactic he had always used with his gang. Fear was his greatest weapon to make them obey him and gather the information he needed. Fulgur didn't like what even the son of Senator Julius Claudius might confess under arrest about what he had discovered in the Colosseum.

Fulgur hurried around the block. On the other side of the villa, near the side door—still no one. They had all disappeared, the scoundrels! And to think he had trusted them!

Fulgur carefully eyed the surroundings. He had to get inside. He had to know, had to figure out what was going on. It didn't take him long to find the alleyway where he could get up to the roof without being seen. Fulgur entered the alley. The smell was disgusting, but Fulgur didn't care. The truth was, he didn't care about anything. He was like a rock, unmovable. Nothing got to him. Nothing, except when anyone disobeyed him. Then he was furious, savage even.

Fulgur found a foothold on both walls and effortlessly hoisted himself up to the roof. He smiled as he stood back up, pleased with himself: after all these years, he was still as athletic as ever. Unlike all the other former gladiators who had let themselves go, getting fat living the high life, he had kept fit. And he wasn't content, either, with the riches he had piled up thanks to his battles. He wanted more. Always more. He wanted to achieve his dream of a better life, a life far away from here.

He took a look down at Cornelius' patio, eased himself over the parapet, and slithered down to the ground. The house seemed deserted, immersed in total silence. Fulgur scoured the patio with his eyes, and then he did a rapid but methodical search of all the rooms. Nearly the whole house had been turned upside-down. And savagely, it seemed. It didn't take much to guess that the soldiers hadn't found what they were looking for. The boys must have gotten away.

"The idiots!"

Fulgur was thinking about the gang members he had watching the villa: they hadn't even seen the boys leaving the house before the soldiers got inside. They had escaped through the door, no doubt. Or over the roof.

Fulgur was grateful for one thing at least: the boys he was after hadn't spilled the beans yet; otherwise the soldiers would have already raided the Colosseum by now. But it still remained to be seen where they had gone.

XLI

A ROUTINE CHECK

It was useless trying to flee with these dratted mules. But it was just as unthinkable to leave the litter in the middle of the street. It was far too recognizable. It would be child's play to trace it back to its owner, and then from him to Titus. Aghiles looked around, hoping to spot somewhere he could hide Paulus. But, alas, the street was a row of identical houses set squarely and evenly along the edge of the road.

"A security check!" hissed Maximus through the curtain on seeing a soldier approach. He gritted his teeth. This would call for clever chat and imagination. "Let's hope Senator Agrippa's alibi is solid enough," he thought to himself.

The soldier who approached was absurdly little. Aghiles would have made quick work of him if only the rest of the troop weren't so close behind him. Instead, Maximus would have to remain calm and not show the slightest concern.

"Who goes there?" the soldier demanded in a stern voice.

Close up, he looked like one of those ugly, snub-nosed animals the army sometimes used as attack dogs. And, indeed, the man had a flat face, a big fat nose, and a wide forehead with beady little black eyes. His helmet came almost all the way down to his thick eyebrows. His thin lips were pinched in a nasty sneer. He looked ready to bite, making up in overzealousness what he lacked in physique.

"Your names?" he barked.

Maximus swallowed hard and stepped forward. "We're actors."

"Actors…you seem very young for that."

Drat! Maximus hadn't seen that coming. "It's just the makeup," he improvised.

The soldier approached and looked him over. "Are you having a laugh at me? I can't see any makeup on your face."

Maximus stood his ground. With supreme self-assurance, he continued, "That's all the art of makeup, you know. It mustn't be seen."

"And this? What's all this?" he growled, nodding his head toward the litter.

"That's Cleopatra's litter."

The soldier raised an eyebrow. His upper lip rose in a sneer. This young man was clearly making sport of him. And this wasn't the time. Not tonight. He had wanted to be part of the squad headed for the catacombs. To beat up a few Christians. Instead of that, his troop had been assigned normal patrol duties.

"Not the real Cleopatra, of course," Maximus hurried to add. "We're actors. We're going to give a performance, at a private party."

The soldier wrinkled his nose skeptically. He took his time, enjoying making the boy squirm. "Humph! And where would that be?"

"Excuse me?"

"This party!" roared the soldier. "Where is it taking place?"

"Senator Agrippa has invited all the great and the good to his home tonight," Maximus calmly replied, holding his nerve.

That put the soldier on the back foot. He had absolutely no idea who this Senator Agrippa was, but he mustn't let his ignorance show. He gave a little cough and composed himself.

"Senator Agrippa, you say?" he repeated suspiciously.

"The very same."

The soldier looked ill at ease and gave Maximus a doubtful frown. He inspected the lead mule, and then the second. Finally, he approached the litter itself. He walked around it slowly, checking every detail. Night was falling. It was too dark to see through the curtains. So he raised his hand to the cloth. Maximus, Titus, and Aghiles held their breath. The giant Numidian shot a glance to Maximus: at the slightest signal, he would gladly bash the soldier's face in.

The soldier suddenly grabbed both edges of the curtains. Titus took a step forward to stop him, but Maximus held him back. The soldier turned to him with a triumphant smile on his lips and drew the curtains back with a snap.

The look of surprise on his face soon gave way to total embarrassment. His face turned bright red. "Oh! Uh! Excuse me…" he stammered.

He fumbled with the curtains, took a step back, and turned away from the litter. He patted down his uniform, trying to show a little decorum, and returned to Maximus with a sour look. "On your way!" he ordered.

Titus' jaw dropped in amazement, but he was careful not to say a word. Aghiles frowned: something was fishy. Totally bewildered, Maximus still managed to thank the soldier.

With military precision, the soldier quick-stepped back to his troop on the double. When they were sure he was far enough away not to hear them, they each gave a huge sigh of relief.

"What went on there? I don't get it," Maximus confessed.

"Neither do I."

"Unbelievable!"

"What in the world did you do in there to put that man in such a state?" asked Titus, opening the litter's curtains.

Behind the thin cloth, Paulus' face was waxen, but his eyes twinkled with mischief. Next to him, Blandula, her eyes lowered, had gone all pink.

"We made it clear he was interrupting us," replied Paulus with a laugh.

Maximus raised a quizzical eyebrow.

"He discovered us right in the middle of a passionate embrace!"

XLII

VICTOR

Victor wandered aimlessly. He didn't know where to go. Toward the center of the city? Out of the question. He would risk running into one of Fulgur's men. Or even Fulgur himself. Toward the outskirts? Away from Rome? Yes, that might be best. He never really had a place of his own, nowhere to call home. There had been Fulgur's gang, true. But that was all ancient history now.

The streets were almost deserted. Victor had hardly come across anyone. He had noticed a patrol a little while ago. For a brief moment, he wondered if he should just give himself up. Why not, after all? At least he would have a roof over his head for the night. A police cell, yes, but still a roof. But the boy thought better of it. These days, it wasn't a good idea to fall into the hands of the police.

Victor turned down a little side street and suddenly stopped, speechless. An Egyptian litter had pulled up just a few yards in front of him. It was a strange and outrageously gawdy litter covered in gold paint. But that wasn't the only thing that caught Victor's attention. He only had eyes for the three slaves accompanying this bizarre vehicle. One dark-skinned giant, another with curly hair, and a third one, blond and much smaller. His enemies! The ones who had caused his ruin! Victor couldn't believe his eyes. He was back on their trail. Fulgur would be so proud of him! There was no question of letting them get away again. He hesitated a moment, wondering how to proceed. Finally, he made up his mind and flattened himself against a wall to hide. He would follow them. There would be time enough later to work out the best way to inform Fulgur.

XLIII

TRAILED!

In the litter, Paulus had closed his eyes. He wasn't sleeping; all his senses were on the alert, but he didn't want to disturb Blandula, sitting close to him. She was troubled. The kiss they had exchanged had surprised her. It's true, Paulus hadn't really given her any choice. When he realized the soldier was going to inspect everything, he tried to think of a way to hide himself as best he could. The girl's body and long hair looked like the best way to make himself almost invisible. Without a sound, while the soldier was talking to Maximus, he signaled to Blandula to come close. The poor girl was terrified. As she bent over him, he smiled at her and whispered, "Don't be afraid." Then he took her gently by the neck and planted his mouth on her lips. Blandula jumped…but then let herself go, guessing what Paulus was up to. When the soldier opened the curtains of the litter, her tresses covered almost his whole face. The soldier saw nothing but passion!

Maximus was now walking a few steps ahead with a smile on his lips. He was replaying in his mind the soldier's look of embarrassment as he reclosed the curtains. As far as he knew, he had just disturbed two young lovers. Paulus' reaction amused Maximus. His quick thinking had gotten them out of a sticky situation, that's for sure. By kissing Blandula, he passed for a man in perfect health, quite the opposite of what the soldier might otherwise have discovered. Maximus thought again about what Paulus had said that morning, about the Christians' will to live, their determination to remain alive to proclaim Christ's message. He had just given another proof of that.

Maximus gave a backward look at the litter. In the name of all the gods! It really was horribly gawdy! It was a miracle they had gotten through that police check. Maximus could hardly believe it. He looked at Aghiles and gave him a complicit smile. Just at that moment, a few steps behind the Numidian giant, he spotted a man turning into the street; he stopped an instant before crouching back into the shadows. It was only a fleeting glance, but it was enough for Maximus to keep a sharp eye out for trouble. After a few rapid checks, he was sure of it: they were being followed.

"Anything wrong?" asked Aghiles, who had noticed his friend's jumpiness.

Maximus nodded. "Yes, I think so."

He briefly told him how he had been attacked the night before. He didn't go into any details and didn't give Aghiles any time to react. If he hadn't yet told him anything, he said, it was because they had more urgent matters to deal with. "But if one of these people is following me, that could endanger everything," he concluded as calmly as he could.

Aghiles only just stopped himself from immediately turning around to look. "One man on his own?" he asked.

"Apparently."

"Strong?"

"Difficult to say."

"You want me to take care of him?"

Maximus didn't need long to consider. That would lose them time, but he didn't want to risk being followed all the way to the catacombs. "That might be best," he said finally.

"You want me to get him to talk?"

"Yes, I'd like to know who he is and if it was he who attacked me last night."

"Keep going," Aghiles said. "I'll deal with him at the next street corner."

The litter continued on its way as if nothing were the matter. But when they turned down the corner of the next street, Aghiles gave the lead mule a great crack on his rump. The beast immediately broke into a trot, pulling his cumbersome load behind him. Aghiles remained behind. He flattened himself against the wall…and waited.

XLIV

STILL NO ONE

The boy posted at the house of Senator Julius Claudius was starting to get impatient. Very impatient. The boy to relieve him should have arrived by now, but no one had showed up. He wanted to leave; he wanted to go get something to eat. He should have been back to report to Fulgur long ago, but he had been given strict orders: in no case leave the house unwatched. So he didn't dare move.

The boy's eyes suddenly widened. The blood drained from his face. He went white as a sheet. "Fulgur?"

The boss was standing before him with a nasty sneer on his face.

"You didn't show up to report."

The boy gulped.

"I…I…I couldn't. The relief never showed up…"

"No one came to take over the watch?"

"No one."

"How long have you been here?"

The boy shrugged his shoulders.

"It was still daylight when I got here. I haven't moved since then. Just like you ordered."

"Did you see them?"

"Who do you mean?"

"The senator's son and his friends."

175

"No, they haven't come back."

"Are you sure?"

"Certain. I haven't moved."

Contrary to all expectations, Fulgur patted his shoulder in an almost friendly way.

"Good work. It's late. Go home. They won't be back now."

"Are you sure?" asked the boy.

That was one question too many. Fulgur looked daggers at him. He suddenly couldn't stand the boy's naivete and stupidity. Without warning, he went for him and gave him a good thrashing.

XLV

THE AMBUSH

The man following the litter didn't take long to appear at the street corner. He moved silently, keeping to the shadows, staying out of sight. When he saw the litter move ahead, he hastened his pace.

Aghiles waited another few seconds to make sure the man was alone. Then he jumped out behind him. The man hadn't heard or seen a thing. Aghiles' hand came down hard on his shoulder. He turned, looked wide-eyed at Aghiles, and took a punch in the nose before he could even cry out. The boy—for he was in fact just a boy—put his hand up to his bloody face. He stepped back, terrified. He didn't even try to defend himself. He looked about, weighing up his chances of escape. Aghiles, who had been expecting him to put up a fight, looked a little disappointed. A good brawl would have released the tension that had been building up in him all evening. He grabbed the boy's shoulder, almost lifted him off the ground, and dragged him to Maximus.

"Who are you?" asked the senator's son, looking him up and down.

The boy didn't answer.

Curious, Titus went up to him and gave him a long look. Suddenly, he spotted the chain around his neck. "That's mine," he exclaimed.

He jumped at Victor and snatched his *bulla* from the boy's neck. Then he struck out with his fists as he showered him with insults. "You thief! You rotten sewer rat!"

"Titus!" thundered a voice. It was Paulus, who had stuck his head out of the litter.

Titus stopped immediately and turned around. Paulus was giving him a severe look. He seemed older like that.

"What has this person done to you?" Paulus asked.

"He stole my *bulla*!"

"Is that all?"

"It's MY *bulla*! He's a thief!"

Paulus looked at the boy whose nose was still bleeding. "Is that true?" he asked.

The boy nodded his head in silence.

"What's your name?"

"Victor."

"And why did you steal this *bulla*?"

Victor lowered his eyes, looking sheepish. "It looked so beautiful." He made a face.

"But I shouldn't have done it. It's brought me nothing but trouble."

"Trouble?" Paulus' face looked gentle and concerned.

That threw Victor. It was the first time anyone seemed to pay any attention to what he said. Then, suddenly, he told him everything. His life on the streets. Fulgur. The other boys. The thefts in the Forum. The Colosseum. It was a though a dam had burst; the words just flowed out of him.

When he had finished, no one dared speak. It was Maximus who first found his tongue. "You say you had lost our trail?" he asked Victor.

"Yes, I came across you again by chance. I was going to flee the city to get away from Fulgur."

"And this Fulgur's gang, which you're part of, are they still after us?"

"No."

Maximus gave a sigh of relief. "Then let's get going!" he urged the others. "We mustn't run the risk of being spotted again before we get Paulus to safety."

"What about him?" asked Titus, nodding toward Victor.

Maximus bit his lip. Now that he was there, the boy was a hindrance.

"He'll come with me," Paulus said simply.

When no one said anything, he added, "My friends will take him in."

XLVI

AN ENCOUNTER IN THE NIGHT

The litter at last came to a halt. Paulus craned his neck, listening to the noises coming from outside. Next to him, Blandula was afraid to move.

Titus slipped his head through the curtains, making them both jump. "We're here!" he said.

"Hallelujah!" Paulus whispered.

He propped himself up a bit more against the cushions and parted the curtains. When he saw the huge field covered with tombs stretching before him, he was deeply moved. He had known he must come here one day, but he had thought it would be as a corpse, which he had come very close to becoming. Despite his weak state, at that precise moment, Paulus felt more alive than ever. He could feel the blood pulsing through his veins, the nighttime breeze raising the hairs on the back of his neck, the tightness of his skin around his healing wounds.

The litter moved forward another few yards and stopped in the shade of the branches of a weeping willow. It was the ideal hiding place in which to catch their breath and take stock of their surroundings. Blandula leaned outside and shivered. Everything looked so different in the moonlight. She hardly recognized the place.

"Aghiles," whispered Maximus, "where do we need to go?"

The slave too had trouble getting his bearings. "It was at the back, in a dip in the ground," he recalled. He suggested that he scout the grounds. Once the crypt was found, he would come back to get them.

Maximus wasn't happy about splitting up. The simple presence of Aghiles reassured him, and he didn't like the idea of his being out of sight in this strange place. On the other hand, he couldn't go up and down the whole burial place with the litter. It would be too long and hard with the mules. And not discreet enough. As for the idea of carrying Paulus, that was no solution either. At that moment, they had no time to lose. Up till then, they had been lucky, but how long would their luck hold out?

"Hurry up!" he said. "The longer we're split up, the more dangerous it will be."

Aghiles agreed with a nod. He grabbed Victor by the arm and said, "You, you're coming with me. I prefer it that way."

As he turned to leave, Paulus called to him from the litter. "You need to know the password in case anyone finds you down there," said Paulus. "Remember what happened with Blandula…"

Aghiles went toward the litter. Paulus signaled him to come close and bend down to him before he whispered a few words in his ear, so the others couldn't hear.

"You don't trust us," said Titus, offended.

Paulus shook his head. "No, don't think that. I have every trust in you. What you've done for me is more than enough to earn my eternal gratitude. I'm just trying to protect you."

"You?! Protect us!?!" Titus snidely retorted. "You? In your state?"

Paulus ignored his sarcasm. "In case you're ever arrested, it's better you don't know the code. They could torture you to get it out of you, and then you'd be suspected of being a Christian."

The very idea gave Titus goose bumps. He lowered his eyes and made no reply. Instead, he pretended to be watching Aghiles as he disappeared from sight among the tombs.

"It's funny," he couldn't help remarking after a moment. "It doesn't look anything like other cemeteries I've seen. There aren't even any funeral pyres burning."

"We don't burn our dead," said Paulus. "We bury them, for we believe our bodies will rise again."

"What an idea! So the lame will come back lame again?" asked Maximus sarcastically.

Paulus smiled. "On that day, I'm sure the Lord will have remedied some of our little defects."

Maximus shrugged his shoulders and looked into the distance. Aghiles was gone. He was nowhere to be seen.

Just at that moment, Dux began getting excited in the litter. He climbed onto Blandula's shoulder, slid back down, climbed onto Paulus' head, came back down again, and turned back to Blandula.

"Calm down, Dux," she said to the monkey in a gentle voice.

But the animal became more and more agitated. He stuck his head under one of the blankets. That made Blandula laugh. But then, he suddenly jumped from the litter onto Titus' shoulder and hid himself around his neck.

"Dux! What's going on?"

The two mules were also becoming jittery.

"Whoa! Whoa there!" said Titus, trying to calm the animals.

Maximus turned and signaled to Titus to keep quiet. Like all animals, Dux and the mules had more heightened senses than people. Clearly, they were sensing something.

Maximus, Titus, Paulus, and Blandula strained their ears. It was Titus who heard it first. Just a few yards away from the weeping willow. Then Blandula, Maximus, and Paulus heard it too. Footsteps. The four young people listened in silence. Without a sound, Paulus sank further down into the cushions and covered himself with a sheet. Blandula laid down next to him to make it look like she was alone in the litter. Maximus and Titus looked around them for a stick or anything they could use as a weapon.

But there was nothing. The willow branches were light and supple. Maximus knelt and inspected the ground with his fingertips. When he found a stone that seemed a good size, he grasped it and stood up.

The noise was coming closer and closer. Dux slipped inside his master's tunic. Maximus' knuckles tightened around the stone. Titus gritted his teeth, trying to restrain the two mules straining at their harness.

Suddenly, the willow branches moved slightly. Maximus readied his arm. After what seemed an eternity, there was a grunt in the bushes. Maximus lowered his arm and gave a sigh of relief.

"A pig!" said Titus, feeling silly. "No need to worry."

But his relief was short-lived. It was in fact a wild boar. An enormous one. Followed by its two little piglets.

"A mother boar with her young!" exclaimed Maximus. "Quick! Climb!"

Wise advice: mother boars with their young were known to become very aggressive. In one bound, Maximus was at the tree trunk, grabbing hold of the first branch he could find. Then he easily clambered up a few yards above the ground. He was out of reach of the boar. But Titus, on the other hand, hadn't been quite as quick. He had headed for the tree, but the mother boar was already blocking his way. Without thinking, he jumped onto the back of one of the mules, which brayed in fright.

184

The poor beast of burden wasn't the only one surprised. Its cry of terror froze the boar to the spot. The mule's continued brays of indignation attracted the boar's attention. After what seemed endless moments summing up the threat, the animal clearly decided Cleopatra's litter was an enemy too big for her. It's true, it was quite a sight. The boar suddenly gave a grunt, pushed her little ones before her with her snout, and trotted away.

Titus heaved a sigh of relief. He leaned down over the mule's neck and hugged it in gratitude.

"Let's hope this will all soon be over!" said Maximus.

XLVII

DISAPPOINTMENT

Aghiles smiled with relief as he spotted the entrance to the crypt. He moved forward slowly, straining his ears for the slightest sound. He gave a sharp signal to Victor to follow him. But he needn't have worried; Victor was far too terrified by this place to try any funny business.

Aghiles walked ahead, careful to tread noiselessly. When he reached the entrance, he whispered the password that Paulus had given him. No reply. He put his foot on the top step of the stairs and repeated the code. Still no response. Aghiles took a deep breath. He didn't like this one bit. He felt danger lurking. He readied himself. He tried the password a third time, but still nothing. Behind him, Victor hardly dared to breathe.

After a little hesitation, Aghiles decided to plunge ahead further down into the crypt. After all, what choice did he have? He went down another few steps, on the defensive, his fists raised, ready to do battle. But when he got to the bottom of the stairs, still no one had appeared. He was greeted by nothing but a deep and icy silence.

Aghiles had thought he would come across a guard or a watchman to whom he could entrust Paulus. Instead of that, the place seemed strangely empty; it was full of a nauseating stench that Aghiles couldn't identify. He felt along the wall, recalling that the blind man had found a torch there. With a little luck, there would also be a lighter somewhere nearby so he could see more clearly. The torch-holder was empty. But the lighter was still hanging on a nail. Aghiles grabbed it and felt his way further along the wall.

As he moved forward, his toe hit something on the ground. Aghiles bent down and reached out his hands. With his finger-tips, he felt a thick piece of wood soaked in what must be water…but thick, gooey water. He realized it was the handle of the torch. He grasped it and worked the lighter. After a few tries, he managed to ignite the moist fabric of the torch.

Aghiles blinked several times, blinded by the bright flame, and moved the torch around him. Victor gave a little cry. There, on the wall, was a bloody handprint. Aghiles shivered at the sight of the pool of blood on the ground that the torch had been sitting in. He suddenly understood: that stench was the smell of blood. Someone had been beaten here, and savagely. What had happened to those who had been guarding the place? Had they fled? Were they dead? Imprisoned? It was impossible to know. Aghiles didn't wait to find out; he ran out of the crypt, the torch still in hand. There was no point putting it out now: there was no one left to see him. And it might just come in handy.

XLVIII

ARREST

Flavia's brother was in a mad rush. He hadn't even bothered returning to the barracks to change his blood-stained uniform. He must find his sister; he had to make sure she was still alive. He hoped he would find her at the home of Senator Julius Claudius. He knew she went there most evenings.

The soldier forced back his tears; he felt like he was going to be sick. His head swam with horrible images that made him want to scream. If only his troop had just been sent to patrol the streets as usual! The things he had just seen happen in the catacombs were horrible, unbearable. He had never seen such bloodthirsty hatred on the part of his fellow soldiers. Such needless violence. Such fury against those poor people who had nothing but sticks to defend themselves. Flavia's brother hoped his sister's god was as good and loving as she never ceased telling him. If not, what had been the point of so much suffering on the part of the defenseless?

When he reached the corner of the dead-end street leading to the senator's villa, he spotted a man violently kicking a figure on the ground. The soldier squinted. It looked like a lifeless body. It was the same blind hatred he had witnessed earlier, the same murderous madness against the weak. It was more than the soldier could stand in one evening. His blood boiled. He lunged at the man.

In his fury, Fulgur hadn't heard him approach. When he raised his head, it was too late. The point of the soldier's sword was already at his throat.

Fulgur had known too many fights to the death not to understand that this man wasn't kidding. He could read it in his icy stare. He heard it in his tone of voice, cold and determined. Above all, he felt it in the pressure of the blade against his neck. One single move from him, and the soldier would carry out his threat and kill him.

"Get up!" said the soldier as he stuck his weapon a little harder against Fulgur's skin. A drop of blood trickled from the tiny wound.

Fulgur raised his hands and slowly rose. The game was up. And Fulgur knew it.

XLIX

THE END OF THE JOURNEY

When he noticed the glint of the torch approaching them, Maximus heaved a sigh of relief. At last, help was on the way. Paulus' friends would be taking charge of him, and Maximus and his friends could finally get back to normal life.

But Aghiles and Victor were alone.

"There's no one there," said the Numidian with a stony face. "And there are signs of fighting."

Paulus went pale. "Fighting?"

"I found blood."

"Dear Lord," Paulus murmured.

There was no need to say more. They could all easily imagine what must have gone on in the crypt… and the consequences there would be.

After a long silence, Paulus at last spoke. "You've done everything you could for me. Leave me here."

As one, they all turned to him. What Paulus suggested caught them by surprise. It was madness, so senseless after everything they had been through. But, before any of them had the time to object, Paulus went on.

"I know what a risk you've taken because of my presence among you," he said. Turning to Maximus, he added, "I am infinitely grateful to you for having dared to save me when all your instincts told you to abandon me."

Maximus lowered his eyes in embarrassment.

Then Paulus looked at Titus. "And you, you moved heaven and earth for me…" To Aghiles he said, "And you, you carried me…"

And then, to Blandula, "You nursed me, fed me, and washed me." After looking each of them in the eye, he concluded, "You all have come to my aid. Without you, I would be dead. But now you must leave me. If you stay, your lives are endangered. Blandula already can no longer go home. This must end here."

Maximus stared at his sandals. Out of all of them, he understood best what Paulus was saying: he couldn't go on indefinitely slipping through the net that was inevitably closing around him, a Christian. They had already been so fortunate: The mysterious way Paulus had escaped when Cornelius' house had been searched. Their journey across Rome with Cleopatra's litter without getting caught. There was no point tempting fate any longer.

"Maximus!" said Paulus, snapping him out of his thoughts. "Maximus, I want you to go. I'll manage; don't worry."

"But you're so weak."

"I'll stay with him," Victor piped up. "I have no place to go anyway."

Paulus smiled. "You see, the Lord has not forsaken me!" Then he fixed his eyes on Blandula. "I entrust Blandula to your care," he said to Maximus. "Make sure she finds a roof over her head, and quickly!"

Maximus gave a solemn nod of his head. Aghiles took the girl's hand and squeezed it. Titus gave a little cough to hide his emotion. Then Paulus made a sign to Aghiles for his help. The giant Numidian approached, took him by the shoulders and the legs, and gently raised him up. Paulus was so light. He laid him under the weeping willow. Blandula had tears in her eyes and was fighting back her sobs. She brought him a toga as well as Master Cornelius' Gospels.

"No, keep them," Paulus told her.

"But I can't read."

"Maximus will read them to you."

He grabbed the scroll and unrolled it a little. He asked Titus to bring the torch a little closer so he could read. When he found the passage he was looking for, he closed the scroll and handed it to Blandula. "Take care of it," he told her. "And read that text, in remembrance of me."

Then, he suddenly became impatient to put an end to these overlong farewells.

"Go! Go on! Leave! It's time."

Each of them paused a moment. Just before leaving him, Aghiles handed the torch to Victor and said, "You need it more than we do."

"To help watch out for boars," Titus added. "May Jupiter protect you!"

Paulus nodded and watched them go. By way of a farewell, the mule at the back of the litter gave a long hee-haw before disappearing through the foliage.

They had hardly gone a few yards before Maximus turned to his slave. "Aghiles, please, stay here. Watch out for him from a distance. He mustn't know you're there. Check that nothing bad happens to him. I want to be sure Victor does him no harm."

Aghiles didn't need to be told twice. After a quick nod of the head, he went back and disappeared into the night.

L

NO NEWS

Worry gnawed at Maximus. It was three days ago now that he had asked Aghiles to stay close to Paulus, and there was still no news. His slave hadn't returned, and Maximus had heard rumors that there had been more arrests among the Christians. That was inevitable after the soldiers' raid of the catacombs. There had been many prisoners taken—and many deaths as well—and torture had, alas, loosened many tongues.

"Still nothing?" Blandula asked Maximus as he crossed the patio of his family villa. The boy had managed to have Blandula taken into her parents' household. It hadn't been too difficult as his mother had been immediately impressed by the girl. She had even insisted that Blandula be appointed to her personal service.

"No," grumbled Maximus.

"Everything will work out fine, I'm sure of it."

Blandula's confidence amazed the boy. And when he asked her how she could be so certain, she just shrugged her shoulders, unable to reply. She just knew it, that's all. It was almost as though Paulus' calm, despite his alarming condition, had rubbed off on her. She wasn't in the least worried, only a little impatient. She wanted to know everything had gone well.

Suddenly, they could hear exclamations at the house door. Maximus quickly turned his head, full of hope. When he spotted his friend's tall figure approaching, he ran to him.

"By Jupiter," he exclaimed, "where have you been?!" He scolded him affectionately, trying to hide his joy. He was terribly relieved to see him again. Aghiles smiled. He was exhausted but happy to be home again.

"Tell us! Tell us what happened!" Blandula begged him.

"I need to wash first," he replied simply.

Heedless of their pleas, he turned on his heels, and swaying with fatigue, headed straight for the slaves' quarters. He was so covered in dust and mud, his hair looked gray.

Blandula and Maximus watched him go, and then looked at each other.

"You were right," said Maximus. "I should have had faith. I'll send for Titus. He'll want to hear Aghiles' story too."

Several hours later, Aghiles at last reappeared on the patio. Blandula, Maximus, and Titus were there waiting for him, trying to pass the time as best they could, playing jacks with little bones.

"Excuse me," Aghiles apologized. "I fell asleep."

Titus stood and greeted him warmly. "My friend! At last, you're back!"

Aghiles simply smiled: he had never been any good with shows of emotion.

"So?!" Maximus asked him.

"What about Paulus?" Blandula wanted to know.

"Everything's fine," Aghiles said. "Paulus is safe." He would have happily stopped there, but that wouldn't satisfy his friends' curiosity. At least this once he needed to be a little more talkative.

"I did as you asked me, Maximus," he told them. "I went back and hid, and kept an eye on Paulus' hiding place…"

LI

THE GOOD SAMARITAN

"The hours crept slowly by," Aghiles continued. "I think I must have fallen asleep. At dawn, I woke with a start. I smelt something funny. Like something burning. I jumped up and saw smoke coming out from under the weeping willow. Paulus was deep asleep. Victor too. In his sleep, he had dropped the torch. The fire was taking hold of Paulus' toga. I stamped out the flames, which woke Paulus.

"'Aghiles!' he said, 'What are you doing here?'

"'I'm looking out for you. Maximus told me to keep watch.'

"Paulus said nothing. I could tell he wasn't very pleased that you hadn't listened to him. But, on the other hand, since I'm strong… We spent most of the morning under the willow tree. As soon as we heard a vehicle, a horse and some men approaching, we curled up as small as we could in order not to be seen."

"You? Small?" Blandula giggled.

Aghiles nodded. "Well, in any case, no one saw us. I didn't know what Paulus wanted to do. I think he needed a little time to think. Or perhaps, to pray. He kept murmuring something into his beard. Then, around noon, he finally said, 'If I don't get out from under this willow tree now, I'll be here forever.'

"So Victor and I carried him to the edge of the road. He hoped someone would take pity on him. I didn't like that very

197

much, but I didn't have any other ideas. So I went back and hid again.

"I waited a long time. A lot of people went past Paulus, but none of them even slowed down when they saw him. No, they all hurried by even more quickly. I have to admit, he was a frightening sight, so skinny he looked at death's door.

"But at last, one man stopped. He was leading a cartload of hay. He went up to Paulus and they exchanged a few words. Then the man clasped Paulus by the shoulders and Victor took his feet, and they laid him in the cart amid the hay. Victor climbed in too. As they left, Paulus gave a little wave to bid me goodbye. He didn't know where I was hiding."

"And you left him like that?" asked Blandula.

Aghiles shook his head. "No, I followed him. All the way to the home of the man with the cart. When they got there, he called for some help. Two boys—his sons, I suppose—came to carry Paulus inside."

"But why haven't you come back till now?" Maximus asked. "I've been worrying about you for three days!"

"I waited a little longer to make sure everything was all right."

"And?"

"Yesterday, Paulus came out of the house. Victor was helping him to walk."

Blandula smiled. "He's all right, then?"

Aghiles nodded his head. "He and Victor looked like old friends. I wouldn't be surprised if Paulus is leading Victor to God."

"What makes you say that?"

"Nothing special. It was just the feeling I got."

"Oh, so now you're a fortune-teller too, are you?" retorted Titus, with a little touch of sarcasm.

198

The three friends looked from one to another with pleased expressions on their faces. They could be proud of what they had done. They had saved a life.

"Good. That's very good," Maximus murmured.

"When I left him, Paulus asked me to remind you about the passage in the book of Blandula's master. Have you read it?" asked Aghiles.

Maximus shook his head. He had completely forgotten about it. When he had returned home after their adventure, he had hidden the book in a corner of his room and given it no more thought. He rose to go get it. He returned with it hidden under a fold of his tunic to avoid attracting anyone's attention.

Then the four friends gathered in the corner of the patio and listened as Maximus read aloud:

> And behold, a lawyer stood up to put him to the test, saying, "Teacher, what shall I do to inherit eternal life?"
>
> He said to him, "What is written in the law? What do you read there?"
>
> And he answered, "You shall love the Lord your God with all your heart, and with all your soul, and with all your strength, and with all your mind; and your neighbor as yourself."
>
> And he said to him, "You have answered right; do this, and you will live."
>
> But he, desiring to justify himself, said to Jesus, "And who is my neighbor?"
>
> Jesus replied, "A man was going down from Jerusalem to Jericho, and he fell among robbers, who stripped him and beat him, and departed, leaving him half dead. Now by chance a priest was going down that road; and when he saw him he passed by on the other side. So likewise a Levite, when he came to the place and saw him, passed by on the other side.

But a Samaritan, as he journeyed, came to where he was; and when he saw him, he had compassion, and went to him and bound up his wounds, pouring on oil and wine; then he set him on his own beast and brought him to an inn, and took care of him. And the next day he took out two denarii and gave them to the innkeeper, saying, 'Take care of him; and whatever more you spend, I will repay you when I come back.'

"Which of these three, do you think, proved neighbor to the man who fell among the robbers?"

He said, "The one who showed mercy on him."

And Jesus said to him, "Go and do likewise."[1]

"That's strange," said Titus. "It's almost as though Paulus knew what was going to happen with the man in the hay cart."

"Oh, no," Aghiles exclaimed. "He told me this text was about us…"

---

1. Luke 10:25-37, RSV, 2CE

EPILOGUE

A few days later…

Titus, Maximus, and Aghiles were in the thermal baths when a noise echoed through the cavernous building. Not far from the Forum and the Colosseum, the baths were a popular meeting place for Romans. They gathered there for sports or relaxation, or to consult the books freely available in the library there. Whether in the hot thermal baths of the caldarium or the icy baths of the frigidarium, the entire city met there to talk and gossip about the latest.

And that day, there was breaking news. Word had only just arrived and was circulating from one room to another, and from one pool to another. Some men hopped out of the water to dress rapidly and find out what the chatter was outside.

"What's going on?" Maximus asked the man next to him, who was clucking with excitement after a long chat with his neighbor.

"Apparently, the Roman police made a raid on the Colosseum!"

"The Colosseum?"

"Yes."

"But the Colosseum is empty! There aren't any games on at the moment."

The man smiled. He was savoring the effect of his next bit of news before springing it on Maximus. He couldn't help it; he loved surprises.

"Well, that's what everyone thought. But, listen to this: an organized gang had set up headquarters there!"

"No!" Maximus feigned surprise to perfection. Aghiles couldn't hold back a smile as he watched his friend enjoying the situation.

The man wagged his head. His chubby cheeks were pink with delight. "Incredible, isn't it? I only just heard."

A messenger came running up. "Senator!" he called. "Senator Agrippa!"

The man with whom Maximus had been speaking turned. The three boys were wide-eyed with amazement.

"A-grip-pa!" Titus mouthed in silence.

Maximus nodded with hilarity. So here was the man who had given them their alibi without even knowing it! Maximus had imagined someone refined and elegant who liked dazzling his guests. Instead, the senator was a fat little man with a rosy complexion and an open, outgoing air. Someone who clearly enjoyed life. As the messenger whispered in his ear, the man looked at Maximus, his eyes sparkling with excitement.

"They've arrested about thirty men," he announced triumphantly. "They were squatting in the workmen's quarters."

"I knew it!" Titus blurted out.

"Pardon?"

Titus turned his head and waved his hand in front of him. "Nothing, nothing! Excuse me."

"About thirty men, you say?" Maximus continued.

But they were again interrupted by a new arrival who couldn't help blurting his news out loud. "There's talk that it's a former gladiator who was the gang leader."

"A gladiator?" asked one man.

"Someone called Fulgur."

"Fulgur?" asked Senator Agrippa in astonishment.

"Why? Do you know him?" asked Maximus.

"In two ways. In his day, he was a famous gladiator, but no one ever heard what became of him."

"And then?"

"Sorry?"

"You said in two ways."

"Yes, indeed. He was arrested by a soldier last week."

This time, Maximus was truly surprised. "Arrested?" he asked, not without a certain relief.

"Yes. But he jumped on the soldier's sword before he could be taken to prison. He died on the spot." Senator Agrippa smiled in satisfaction at the effect of his news. "Aren't our soldiers wonderful?" he asked with enthusiasm. "They've got their nose to the ground!"

"Hmm…nothing gets past them," Maximus added with a knowing smile. He took leave of the imposing senator and headed for the other end of the pool. All over, the baths were buzzing with the news. He strained his ear to hear and, suddenly, a few words caught his attention. He smiled with amusement and went to find Aghiles and Titus.

"What incredible news," he whispered to them with a mischievous wink. "I just heard the police were acting on an anonymous tip-off. Who would have believed it?"

Printed in June 2020 by Rotolito, Italy
Job number MGN 20020
Printed in compliance with the Consumer
Protection Safety Act, 2008